BACK-SHOOTER!

Only the sporadic shifting and swaying of the train saved him. Bill was hurrying along a narrow plank walkway, toward the ladder at the back of the last caboose, when a rough section of railbed below sent him stumbling hard.

At the very moment he pitched sideways, a gun barked behind Bill, and he felt a sharp tug as the bullet passed through the folds of his shirt under the left armpit.

By long necessity, Bill's reflexes were primed against back-shooters. Rather than recover from his stumble, Hickok let himself drop, even as a second bullet creased his back like a tongue of fire licking him.

Hickok tucked, rolled hard, and prayed he wouldn't run out of rolling room on the narrow railcar. The lithe frontiersman came up in a squatting position at the very edge of the roof, already fanning his hammer.

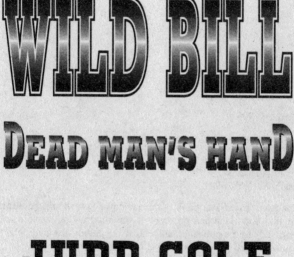

WILD BILL

DEAD MAN'S HAND

JUDD COLE

LEISURE BOOKS NEW YORK CITY

A LEISURE BOOK®

February 1999

Published by

Dorchester Publishing Co., Inc.
276 Fifth Avenue
New York, NY 10001

ISBN 0-8439-4487-0

DEAD MAN'S HAND

Chapter One

Joshua Robinson felt nervous butterflies stirring in his belly as he pushed open the slatted bat wings and crossed from the deserted hotel lobby into the raucous saloon.

The fresh-scrubbed youth felt anxious, all right, but also excited and determined, his blood thrumming with the power of all these strange new impressions on his East Coast sensibility.

Josh paused just past the entrance, turning his bowler hat nervously around in his hands while he tried to get his bearings. A pall of blue smoke hung over the huge, high-ceilinged room, so thick it had no room to move and just hung there like bunting. An S-shaped mahogany bar snaked along the far side of the room, with two barkeeps in sleeve garters and string ties hustling to serve a demanding crowd. A huge back-bar mirror doubled the occupants of the room. It was more people than Josh had seen in any one place since coming west of the Mississippi River three days earlier.

"God Almighty!" the youth breathed, too awestruck to do anything but stand there. He'd seen it all before in a hundred dime novels. But now Josh understood—looking at a map of France was nothing like visiting Paris.

His eyes searched the motley crowd, looking for a face he had never actually seen but could draw in the dark from memory, for Josh had studied every known photograph or drawing of the bigger-than-life figure he had come to meet.

The men at the crowded bar represented every social stratum and occupation, from lowly buffalo-skinners to wealthy cattle buyers. Denver, once a little mining camp called Cherry Creek, now boasted it was becoming "the Chicago of the high plains." These men were dressed in everything from fringed buckskins to the "reach-me-downs" produced by America's thriving new ready-to-wear industry. Josh felt a special thrill of excitement at all the weapons in evidence. No one back in Philadelphia carried firearms, not even the city roundsmen who kept the peace.

The youth's eager eyes cut to the right side of the big saloon, where well-dressed men were playing games of chance at a scattering of green-baize card tables.

There! There he was, coming down the rear stairway.

"Man alive!" Josh said out loud, but softly. "It's really him!"

"Boy, you best clean your ears or cut your hair!" growled a voice like rough gravel behind Josh. "I said stand away from the damn door, you gaping mooncalf! Make room for your betters!"

A hand like a steel trap gripped Josh's shoulder and threw him roughly to one side. He crashed hard into a heavy table and barely caught himself before he sprawled headlong to the floor.

Sudden anger made his temples throb. Josh glanced left, into the bearded, grinning face of one of the meanest-looking hardcases he had ever seen. The man reeked of rotgut and had little, piglike eyes set close together. Lumps of old scar tissue around his eyes betokened plenty of bare-knuckle brawling.

Josh somehow managed to force the words past the lump of fear in his throat. "Mister, you had no call to lay a hand on me. Nor to insult me."

"Well now, she talks!" the bearded bully exclaimed, taking in Josh's new wool suit and glossy ankle boots. "And lookit how her little chin quivers when she gets riled! You'll pipe down, you damned little barber's clerk, or next time I'll cowhide you."

"Baylis!" snapped a clear, imperious female voice behind Josh. "Do your duties for my fiancé include picking on children? Leave that lad alone!"

Despite his excitement about finally spotting the legend he came to see, Josh suddenly had eyes only for the young vision of beauty who now stepped into the saloon. She looked curiously about her, as if entering an exotic square in Persia.

"Oh, Randolph!" she cried out to someone behind her in the lobby. "It's positively *breath*taking! So much grim masculinity! Is *this* how you lucky men spend your time when you're away from your wives and sweethearts?"

"This is your lucky day, boy," the hardcase named Baylis muttered to Josh. "The old man's fancy woman takes pity on weak things. But I'll settle your hash later."

9

The woman who had called Josh a child was in fact, he decided quickly, no older than he was. He stared openly and boldly at her as she surveyed the big room. Lord God, but she was a beauty! The pale, mother-of-pearl skin, those pronounced cheekbones—she was Josh's ideal of Spanish royalty. A gay ostrich-feather boa was draped loosely around slim white shoulders. But Josh glimpsed an exciting plunge of cleavage where tight stays thrust her breasts up prominently.

She smiled at him briefly while Baylis swaggered up to the bar, hitching his Levi's. His eyes stayed in constant sweeping motion, like those of payroll guards. Josh noticed that his hand-tooled holster was tied down with a rawhide whang.

A second man emerged through the bat wings and took the young woman protectively by one elbow.

"Elena," he said, his suave baritone sharp with disapproval, "this is not a good idea, I tell you. *Your* kind of woman doesn't enter such places. Only singers and soiled doves."

She tossed back her pretty head and laughed, showing Josh even little teeth white as pearls. "*My* kind of woman may not do *any*thing," she pouted. "Darling, you promised! We agreed I was to come west with you this trip and have a real frontier adventure before I become an old married lady. Besides—it's safe. Baylis is watching in case any of these men should . . . lose control."

"Don't be coarse," the man named Randolph snapped irritably. "Besides, I don't require Baylis to protect you."

This new arrival, Josh guessed, was at least twice the girl's age. His hair was silver at the temples and his sharp face slightly puffy and lined. Despite his fine tailoring, he had the smug, self-satisfied air of what Josh's mother primly called "new money."

The man finally noticed Josh gawking at his fiancée and frowned at the youth. "You lose your home, sonny?" he demanded. "Or are you looking for someone?"

"I found him," Josh replied, taking one last, approving look at the pretty Elena. Then the youth picked up his hat from the floor, dusted it off, and headed back toward the card tables at the rear of the saloon.

The man he had come more than 1,600 miles to find was returning from the bar, carrying a bottle of Old Taylor bourbon and a pony glass. He walked a bit stiff-legged, and Josh felt proud for knowing exactly why: In 1866, while on an extended scout in western Kansas for Custer and Sheridan, his horse was shot out from under him. His left foot got hung up in a cinch, and the horse went down on his leg, crushing it.

All the photographs, Josh decided, did not do the living man justice. He was somewhere in the prime years just after 30, exceptionally handsome if somewhat of a "fashion dandy," quiet in manner but with an air of possessing deep reserves of inner strength. Nothing about his manner suggested the frontier bully, yet most bullies surely gave him a wide berth. For the man's confidence in himself was palpable.

The man scraped back a chair and was about to sit down at a table of poker players. Then

Josh watched him glance back and notice a doorway behind that chair.

"Excuse me, friend," Josh heard him say politely to one of the players. "May I trade places with you? My eyes aren't what they used to be. I need to be closer to the light."

Josh knew all that was a smoke screen. He watched the speaker settle into a chair facing the doorway. This new spot also left the man with an excellent view of the entire room.

Josh swallowed a nervous lump and stepped closer to the table, remembering his plan of action. "Excuse me, gentlemen. My name is Joshua Robinson, and I am not a cardplayer. But with your permission, may I watch?"

The man Josh had come to meet just ignored him, frowning over his cards. But an older man with a soup-strainer mustache looked up at the youth curiously.

"The hell for, son?"

"I . . . I've read that a man can learn to play poker, monte, and faro just from watching others, sir. And *no* man ignorant of cards need bother going west."

That comment finally caused the handsome dandy in the long blond curls to glance up at Josh for a moment, squinting a bit in speculation. It should have, Josh thought. *He's* the very gent who first said that.

The older man shrugged one shoulder. "Boy, you haven't even grown into that new hat yet. But you speak up like a man. G'wan, pull up a chair. But no spirits and nary a peep, hey?"

"Yes, *sir*, I promise."

The game went quietly forward, cards slapping the green baize, chips clinking. Josh looked away long enough to check on the hard-case, Baylis. He was nursing a bottle at the bar while the rich man named Randolph escorted Elena around the saloon, pointing out such details as the new player piano and the war bonnets mounted on the walls. When the seated male customers spotted Elena on Randolph's arm, they came hastily to their feet, doffing hats and many bowing gallantly.

"Oh look, darling!" Josh heard her exclaim. "Those men are gambling!"

Hearing a woman's voice nearby, the players at the isolated tables glanced up in surprise. As the couple drew nearer, the men at Josh's table rose politely to their feet, Josh included.

All, that is, except the handsome man frowning over his cards. "I'll take three, damnit," he muttered to the dealer, ignoring the new arrivals and all the sudden fuss around him.

"Sir!" Elena called out gaily, her voice more teasing than censorious. "You are the best-dressed man at the table, yet no gentleman, I see."

Still mulling his cards as if they'd betrayed him, the man replied absently, "Madam, you are quite beautiful and clearly right out of the top drawer. But you see, I am a man fixed in his little habits. I stand up to pee, lie down to sleep or make love, and *sit* when I'm playing cards. Right now, as you may observe, I'm playing cards."

Josh watched his eyes flick up to meet the woman's as he added pointedly, "Although I *might* be talked into changing my position."

His innuendo was clear, and Elena blushed to her very earlobes. Randolph flushed with rage. Before he could get himself under control to speak, a likewise offended young cowboy, clearly well into his cups, came blustering closer.

"Listen, mister," he said loudly. "This here is a *lady*. I don't know what hole you crawled out of, but here in Denver we respect a lady."

"Three cards," the man repeated to the dealer, still ignoring all the commotion. The young puncher was about to move in even closer when a friend suddenly gripped his arm and said something in his ear. He pointed toward the seated player. Josh saw that the man's coattails had dropped open, revealing two Colt .44s with fancy pearl grips.

The cowboy looked closer at the man's calm, fathomless eyes and neatly trimmed mustache. And abruptly he realized his big mistake.

"Pardon me all to hell, Mr. Hickok," the cowboy stammered. "There's no offense meant."

"Nor none taken," James Butler "Wild Bill" Hickok assured him quietly. He fished into the fob pocket of his vest and flipped the cowboy two bits. "Go have a drink on me, waddie. She's a fine lady, and you were right to stick up for her."

To verify this, and pour oil on the waters, Hickok rose, bowed graciously, and sat down again to his cards. But Josh had noticed something: the moment the cowboy said "Mr. Hickok," Baylis almost dropped his glass. Now Josh saw him slide his six-shooter from its holster and cover it with his hat. That's when Josh remembered there was an open bounty— $10,000 in gold double eagles—on Hickok, the legacy of a killing while Bill was marshal of Abilene.

"Wild Bill!" Josh called out. "That man at the end of the bar has a gun aimed at you! It's hidden under his hat!"

At these words, Randolph pulled Elena well out of the line of fire.

"I already know that, son," Bill replied in his quiet way. "But I thank you sincerely for that information. You may still be quite green, but you're solid wood."

Josh flinched hard when Hickok fired from under the table, one deafening shot that drilled Baylis through the heart and spun him off his stool. He hit the floor with a sound like a sack of salt dropping on hardpan. It was so sudden that Elena, although horrified, forgot to scream.

"My apologies, miss," Bill said, holstering his Colt even as men gathered around the body, exclaiming at the accuracy of the shot. "But once a man draws, it's best to shoot him quick."

Hickok's eyes shifted to Elena's flabbergasted fiancé. "I'd wager that . . . man was on your payroll. But don't worry. This city is full of thieves and stinking, murdering bag-line bums like him. I'm sure you'll quickly find a replacement. Check the manure pile at the livery."

Randolph saw how his fiancée was watching Bill, her face frozen in fascination like a bird watching a snake. Josh could tell the wealthy man was fit to be tied.

"I've heard of you, Jim Hickok. Who the hell hasn't? 'Wild Bill' my sweet aunt! You've got every damned ink-slinger in the country selling your supposed exploits to a bunch of gullible greenhorns. I don't credit the lies, not by a jugful. *Some* men don't eat out of your hand."

"That's right," Bill agreed amiably as he again considered his cards. Then he glanced up at Elena, smiled, and added, "Only horses and women do that."

"Now you listen, Hick—"

"No, *you* listen," Bill cut in, his voice going so low it was almost a whisper. "It's no say-so of yours what Jim Hickok does, is it? Don't miscalculate yourself, stranger. That corpse on the floor just overrated himself, too, and it was his last mistake."

Randolph, enraged beyond words now, roughly took Elena by one arm and stormed out. Bill sighed and tossed down his cards. "Call. I've got two pairs: aces and eights."

"Sorry, Wild Billy." The man with the soup strainer chuckled. "Three deuces. You watching this, son?"

Two men were dragging Baylis out while another ran for the undertaker and the sheriff. Hickok looked at the deuces, grimaced, then met Josh's eyes and grinned.

"*When* will I learn to fold on aces and eights, kid? That hand has always been bad luck for me."

Chapter Two

"The *New York Herald,* huh?" Bill Hickok repeated without much enthusiasm.

"Yessir, Wild Bill," Josh said proudly. "The greatest newspaper in America."

"Guess that makes it the Queen of the Crapsheets," Bill said, but so mildly that Josh hardly noticed. The youth had been waiting out front of the Commerce Hotel several hours for this chance; now his words fairly tumbled over each other in his eagerness to explain himself and his purpose while he could.

He told Bill how the newspaper's eccentric publisher, James Gordon Bennett, had never once been west of the Hudson River. Yet the timid soul suffered from the powerful "westering fever" of the 1870s—he even made his outraged wife sleep under buffalo robes instead of eiderdown quilts!

"Mr. Bennett decided to open the nation's first permanent far-west bureau for East Coast newspapers," Josh added. "And I'm it!"

"A nineteen-year-old, wet-behind-the-ears kid," Bill said, still very unimpressed. "Wears a paper collar and doesn't even shave yet. Come to see the big elephant, huh? Does your mother know you're out here?"

While this conversation went forward, Josh

persistent, Bill sarcastic, both men were strolling briskly along the raw-lumber boardwalk of Denver's busy South Platte Street. Vendors with wooden pushcarts hawked honeycombs, sacks of ginger snaps, buffalo tongues pickled in brine. Bill's eyes stayed in constant motion, and he used reflections in plate-glass windows to monitor his surroundings.

"When *you* were nineteen," Josh shot back defensively, "you were elected a constable in Johnson County, Kansas."

"Not wearing a bowler hat, I wasn't. Look, kid, I appreciate that warning you gave me last night. But even if I wanted a sidekick, which I don't, I'd want one that knows gee from haw, at least. C'mon—let's eat."

They ducked into an eating house and Bill treated the young journalist to a hearty meal of beef, biscuits, potatoes, gravy, and greens, with big slices of apple pie for dessert.

"But I wouldn't be your sidekick, Wild Bill," Josh persisted around a mouthful of pie. "I want to tell your story. Yours, and the story of the West—the *wild* West."

"It's wild," Bill shot back, blue eyes flicking regularly to the doors and windows, "about one minute out of every thousand or so. The rest drag by slow, all dull, boring, and hard."

"Not around you! I've already seen you kill a man," Josh reminded him. "And one that deserved it, too. It's plenty wild out here—at least, where you happen to be."

"Most men aren't worth ten thousand dollars dead like I am. You better keep *that* in mind, too, kid. Lead tends to fly around me. You'd be safer back east wearing green eyeshades and squiring the ladies."

While they spoke, a young, unarmed cowboy at the other end of the counter recognized Bill and respectfully approached him, his hand extended. "May I touch you for luck, Wild Bill?"

Bill shook his hand, though he also suggested to the puncher that he lean toward readiness, not luck. Josh hastily scrawled this down in a flip-back pad, and Bill laughed.

"Words, words, words," he muttered. "Look, Longfellow, we're burning daylight and I've got an appointment near the railyard. Good luck to you out west, son. I'll watch for your byline."

Bill threw two silver dollars onto the counter, clapped on his black, broad-brimmed hat, and pushed out into the busy street again. He frowned when Josh followed him like a faithful dog.

"All right if I tag along, Wild Bill?"

Hickok snorted. "You hang on like a tick, don't you? Kid, you're a likely enough fellow. But I'm telling you, I've got no need for you. I travel light, and—"

"*Duck*, Bill!" Josh cut in.

Even as he spun into a doorway, Hickok swept the kid with him, then filled his right hand with a short iron.

"Where?" Bill demanded tersely, still looking for his target. "Spot me, kid! Which one is he?"

"It's not a he," Josh replied. "And you won't need a gun. Look across the street, under the awning of the Song Bird Saloon. I recognized her right off, Wild Bill, from Ned Buntline's descriptions. Especially the hat."

Bill followed Josh's finger, then expelled a

long groan. A stout young woman leaned against the tie rail out front, guzzling whiskey right from the bottle. She had a homely, care-worn face and wore her greasy hair tied in a heavy knot that dangled under an immaculate gray Stetson—the only clean item she had on. A big Smith & Wesson Volcanic pistol was tucked into a bright-red sash around her waist.

"I'll outdrink, outfight, outswear, and out-*shoot* any goddamn white man or Indian!" she roared out in a voice that could fill a canyon.

"Calamity Jane!" Bill swore. "She's found out I'm in Denver. Damn it all! So you know all about her, too, huh?"

"Ain't a man among you!" Jane roared out. "A Sioux papoose has a bigger set on him!"

"Sure," Josh replied eagerly. "Her real name is Martha Jane Burke. But she has sworn on oath to shoot *any* man who calls her Martha. Any man, that is, except the one man in the world she loves: Wild Bill Hickok. She can do it, too. Even you admit she's the best female shootist in America outside of Annie Oakley."

"She is . . . when she's sober. I just wish to God she hadn't set her *romantic* sights on me."

But Josh could see that Bill was looking at him in a new light now, his eyes speculative.

"Kid," Bill said gratefully, "she hasn't got a gun aimed at me, but you just saved my bacon. You know more about me than my mother does. Maybe you and I *could* strike a private treaty."

"You bet we could, Wild Bill! Why, man alive! We could even—"

Bill, busy slipping down an alley now to avoid

Calamity Jane, raised one hand to silence the irrepressible kid.

"Look, slip a noose on this 'we' business. We aren't becoming blood brothers, got it? And you *will* get rid of those damned greenhorn togs you have on. You stick out like a Kansas City fire engine. You own a gun, junior?"

Josh shook his head. "See, my mother was raised Quaker, and I—"

"A fine sect, kid, back in Philly. But there's no Quakers west of Omaha—unless they're good shots. I'll set *thee* up with a barking iron later."

They emerged onto Silver Street, in the shadow of the huge new opera house that made Denver a cut above plain old saloon towns. But Josh also saw proof this was still the rough-and-tumble place his mother feared: An Indian lay motionless in the middle of the street. "Hep! Hep!" shouted a teamster, cracking his long whip and guiding his freight wagon around the sprawled redskin.

Josh goggled at the sight. "Is that Indian drunk, Wild Bill?"

"That or dead," Bill said matter-of-factly. "Listen, kid. Men who survive out here keep their mouths shut and their eyes open. Right now I've got to meet a gent named Allan Pinkerton. He wants to talk with me—privately, if you catch my drift?"

"Pinkerton! Why, he's a detective!"

Bill snorted. "No, he's rich. The detectives take the risks, and that penny-pinching old Scotsman collects the fees."

Josh's eyes widened with gathering excitement. Not even out here a week, and look at all the stories already!

"That's why you came to Denver!" Josh said. "You're hiring on as a Pinkerton man! An operative! *Ho*-ly cow! What is it, Bill? Rustlers? Bank robbers? Maybe counterfeit—"

"Damnit, kid, wouldja caulk up? For now, keep everything I've told you close to your vest, you savvy?"

Josh nodded. "My word of honor."

"That much I'll trust. Now get on back to the hotel and stay out of trouble. I'll look you up later, Longfellow."

At first, Bill assumed Pinkerton had finally gone senile and given him the wrong directions to their meeting place.

Meet me at the big brick dome near the train depot, Pinkerton's telegraph had said. *The one without windows.*

The only building even barely fitting that description turned out to be an icehouse for the storage of winter ice harvested from the nearby Front Range of the Rocky Mountains. But Pinkerton was indeed waiting there for his old friend from the Civil War days.

"Jamie lad!" the old Scotsman greeted him out front, for he wanted nothing to do with the newspapers and this "Wild Bill" nonsense. "You were one of the finest scouts the Union Army ever put in the field. I could never have given General McClellan so much reconnaissance without you."

"Not that Gorgeous George ever *did* anything with it," Bill interjected. "The man had him a brand-spanking-new Army and was afraid to get it dirty."

"It's too dead to skin now, Jamie. But naturally, I thought of you when this latest lucrative assignment recently came up."

"Naturally," Bill repeated scornfully. "That brogue of yours disguises a lot of bullshit, you know that? You old skinflint, what you *really* mean is that nobody else will take the job."

Pinkerton grinned through his white, bushy Burnsides. "Dinna fash yourself, lad! It's an . . . odd assignment, granted. But quite lucrative, I'll assure you."

While he spoke, Pinkerton removed a double-bitted key and unlocked a small door in the brick dome. They stooped to enter a brick-lined area lighted by a single lantern to keep down heat. Neat blocks of ice were stored between insulating layers of sawdust and cheesecloth.

"What do you know about ice, Jamie?" Pinkerton demanded, his breath forming little ghost puffs.

"I know it's *cold*," Wild Bill replied peevishly, slapping his arms to keep warm.

Pinkerton chuckled as he led his friend toward a second door connecting with a smaller chamber.

"Then you have grasped the obvious and missed the essence, I assure you. Young Hickok, I've quite a few years on you. I've seen guns go from flintlock to cap-and-ball to self-contained cartridge repeaters, and I've *still* got some years left, the Lord willing. Jamie, you're going to see things—marvels, laddiebuck!— such as no man can even dream up, not even Jules Verne."

"Al, you always were one for talking like a

book. The hell you jabbering about? It's *cold* in here!"

Pinkerton paused before the second door and nodded his head toward the ice blocks surrounding them.

"That's natural ice, the last of the winter batch. The only ice for hundreds of miles around. It's expensive and already spoken for before it comes out of the mountains. There are precious few icehouses or ice pits west of the Mississippi. Bricks are expensive out here, and digging the pits even more so. They must be fully lined and at least fifty feet deep, and they require complicated grates and drains to handle melt runoff. Only a few of the wealthiest ranches have them."

"R-r-right," Bill said, teeth chattering. "If you wander near a p-p-point, f-f-feel free to make it."

Pinkerton tossed him an old cloth coat hanging from a peg near the door. "The *point*, Jamie, is this: The demand for ice out here, from April through November or so, is absolutely staggering. With ice, meat can be butchered and stored, even shipped. Other perishable foods can be kept indefinitely. Drinks can be cooled, confectioners thrive, a dairy industry can take root."

Pinkerton keyed the lock, still talking.

"But even more important . . . Jamie, when you rode into Denver, did you pass the big pesthouse east of town?"

Bill nodded. Pinkerton meant the huge quarantine center for the latest victims of the scarlet fever plague currently ravaging the city. Bill had smelled the stink of carbolic acid, used to sanitize the streets, even before he reached the city limits.

"Well, once again the pesthouse is full. But this year the *graveyard* isn't. The death rate this year is down eighty percent, Jamie! And I'm about to show you the reason why. But you *mustn't* tell a soul what you're about to see and hear. Your word?"

Bill nodded again, curious in spite of himself. Pinkerton had one hell of a flair for the dramatic.

"All right, then," Pinkerton said, and the lock mechanism snicked when he turned the key. "Prepare yourself, Bill. You've been a soldier, a scout, a spy, a prisoner of war, a U.S. marshal. Seen the big animal again and again. But I assure you—you've seen nothing quite like this before in your life."

Chapter Three

"But, darling! *How* did I 'humiliate' you yesterday?" Elena protested. "He is a very famous man. I was merely taken aback when I realized it was he. This Wild Bill—some say he is the most famous frontiersman in America."

"*He* says that, my love, and the fawning magpies in the press repeat it endlessly in their damnable rags!"

"Why, Randolph! You're jealous!"

"Oh, hogwash! He's nothing, I tell you, Elena. One of Bill Cody's pasteboard cutouts, that's all. My father knew his grandfather Otis Hickok back in Illinois—nothing but common immigrant Irish trash."

"Irish trash, with a deadly aim," Elena reminded Randolph Bodmer. "As Baylis discovered."

Although she had her own room on another floor, as propriety required, Elena had joined her fiancé for coffee and pastry in his huge suite of rooms.

"Even a blind hog," he assured her, "could hit the target at that distance."

"Through the heart across that huge room? A target not only hidden, but as the local paper pointed out, hardly larger than a fist. That—"

"Listen to you!" Bodmer snapped. "You have

an oddly unfeminine zeal, at times, for the morbid. When I say 'humiliate,' I'm talking about the *filthy* way you looked at Hickok, for all to see."

Elena's mother-of-pearl skin colored slightly. " 'Filthy'? A harmless admiring glance?"

"It was a come-hither glance, Elena! Men know these things."

Bodmer dismissed her next protest with an impatient wave. He looked comfortable in a black-and-white striped smoking jacket with velvet lapels.

"You're a beautiful woman, Elena, and God knows I value spirit in a woman as much as I do in a horse. But I have far more ambitious plans than simply getting rich, which I accomplished years ago. I mean to leave my mark on the West! A *deep* mark. That means politics. A beautiful wife can be a real asset to a politico. But if she carries on like a shameless whore of Babylon, she'll sink him fast."

Anger at these words made Elena's nostrils flare. But Bodmer slid the watch from his pocket and thumbed back the cover to check the time. Then he picked up a wallet from the nightstand beside him and removed several banknotes, handing them to Elena.

"Be an angel now and go buy yourself a new hat or some such. I have a business meeting."

Elena tucked the bills into her reticule and crossed to the door, her bustle rustling. With one slim white hand on the glass doorknob, she turned and said:

"Be careful how you accuse me. I just might sin to justify the charges! When you visited my father to ask for my hand, nothing but poetry crossed your honeyed lips. Now my father has passed on, may he rest in peace. You've itemized my dowry, and now I'm compared to the whore of Babylon!"

He started to protest, but she raised a hand to stop him.

"By law, I cannot prevent the marriage now that the banns are published. But by God's holy law, I swear to your execrable face, Randolph, I will *never* share a marriage bed with a contemptible scut like you!"

She slammed the door before Bodmer could recover from this unexpected volley. "Execrable"? He wasn't sure he knew what it meant, but "scut" was clear enough without a dictionary.

Well, spirited women were like thoroughbreds—high-strung and testy. He'd gentle her later with some sugar talk and nice presents. To hell with all this stewing over Hickok. Odds were good they'd never see the arrogant, puffed-up bastard again.

Bodmer tugged a braided pull-rope near the bed, summoning a young porter dressed in red livery. He gave the youth four bits and wrote down a room number at a drifters' boardinghouse near the train station.

"Tell both of the men staying here to come see me at once," Bodmer instructed the porter. "If they're passed out drunk, you'll have to knock a long time to wake them up. But *don't* open the door without permission, hear me? These are very . . . nervous men."

While he waited, Bodmer crossed the luxurious suite and parted the draperies. Ragged clouds obscured the nearby mountain peaks. But he hardly noticed, gazing instead down into the wide, busy street. The panorama made him smile, for he was a businessman and Denver's growth spurt lately truly amazed and delighted him. Last time he had passed through here, on his way to San Francisco, Denver had only one hotel the size of a packing crate.

Now look! This one alone was five stories, with a huge green awning out front and even a damned paved sidewalk, the first in the West. A twelve-foot-wide swath of magnesia limestone that proved *progress* had arrived on the frontier. And progress, Bodmer knew, always meant profits. Especially for those smart enough to move first.

If only, he reminded himself, he could clear the path of all that encumbered it.

As if to underscore this point, three hard knocks sounded on the door.

"It's open," Bodmer called.

Two men entered, one white, one a copper-tinted half-breed. They both took in the textured walls, canopied bed, and gilt mirrors, maintaining that contemptuous silence of lackeys who despised the rich yet needed their patronage.

"Big Bat, Dog Man," Bodmer greeted them, still looking out the window. "There's smooth whiskey in the sideboard, boys. Don't be shy."

"Don't mind if I do cut the dust," replied the white man, Enis "Big Bat" Landry. He was large and barrel-chested, and wore the perpetual sneer of a barracks-room bully. Bodmer knew him as a good marksman but also a deadly expert with a whip. In fact, that lethal skill had Landry on the prod right now: He had bull-whipped a prominent Texan to death after the man caught Landry using a running brand to alter the rancher's "Rocking K" brand.

"Word's all over town," Landry said as he speared the bottle out of the sideboard, "how you had words with Bill Hickok. That straight?"

"What of it?"

"I'll tell you what. He ever gives *me* a clear shot, I'm banking yaller boys! While he was the star-man in Abilene, Hickok killed some mouthy cowboy named Harlan Lofley. Trouble is, *this* mouth had a rich old man who dotes on him. Papa Lofley put up a fat reward. Now Mister Hickok don't sleep so good nights."

"No?" Bodmer said. "He looked well rested to me. But listen up, both of you. Don't get any ideas about gunning for Hickok now. You're supposed to be in my employ as domestics, not a couple of hardened range bums. Don't worry, you'll have other opportunities to brace that son of a bitch. Never mind him for now. Just play along."

Bodmer turned from the window. "I've booked your spots on the train. You'll be traveling in a third-class coach as my domestics."

Big Bat lowered the bottle and wiped his lips on his dirty flannel sleeve. "Third class?" he protested. "How's come we get the crappy end of the stick? You'll be in your own Pullman car, living like the lord of Creation."

Bodmer sneered at both men's greasy, filthy clothing. "It's called social subordination. Water seeks its own level. As does mud."

Big Bat scowled, but Dog Man liked this. His lips pulled back off his teeth in an eerie smile that failed to include the corners of his mouth. The whelp of a Ute mother and a Mexican father, he had eyes like hard black agates.

Rumored to be the best shot between Santa Fe and the Dakota Country, Dog Man took his name from the days when he rode with the Southern Cheyenne renegade Roman Nose, leader of the rebellious Cheyenne Dog Soldier Society. Dog Man's philosophy was simple: Life was a disease, and the only cure was death. Thus, he saw himself as a healer, not a killer.

"I didn't call you here," Bodmer went on irritably, "to discuss your goddamned sleeping arrangements! I want to remind you to keep your eyes out for the main chance. Not only must Professor Vogel meet with a fatal 'accident'—but I *must* have enough time alone with that little Prussian pipsqueak's machine. Time to study and diagram its internal structure before you destroy it. That's absolutely imperative. It's the machine I care about, not Vogel."

It was all quite simple, really, as Bodmer saw things. Vogel had already refused to sell the rights to a patent application for his invention. Bodmer's offer had been generous—very generous. But that soft-brained fool Vogel had refused. Muttering all that malarkey about the "social welfare" being better than profits. Now, Bodmer figured, the normal options were all used up.

"All this," he told his visitors, nodding at the bustling scene below in the street, "hangs by a thread. It might last, and it might not. I've seen boomtowns turn into ghost towns fast. By 1868, Star City, Nevada, was only seven years old—and had only one family left, that of my business representative. A man who means to get on in new country must move quickly and decisively."

Big Bat drained the whiskey, smacked his lips, and dropped the empty bottle, letting it thunk harmlessly on the thick carpet.

"Boss," he said. "No offense to you personal. But I need all your philosophy like a boar hog needs tits! I'm here on account I'm light in the pocket and need paying work. Same with the Dog Man. You pay four dollars a day, and chumley, that beats hell out of thirty a month and grub for nursing beeves."

Big Bat paused to belch, then added: " 'Sides all that, they's a hemp committee back in Texas, and the rope waitin' on me has got thirteen coils in it. So you just tell us who needs killing, and we'll plant 'em, no questions asked."

Chapter Four

Bill forgot about the cold after Pinkerton opened the second door and they stepped inside the innermost storage chamber of the icehouse.

A small, thin, flat-chested old man with a wild tangle of fine white hair stood beside a . . . clumsy metal box, Bill decided. Or more like a metal cabinet on four squat legs. The old man ignored the new arrivals. He muttered incessantly to himself as he tinkered with a set of equations in a handheld ledger.

But what truly dropped Bill's jaw in astonishment were all the glittering chunks of ice spewing out of a chute on one side of the cabinet. Chunks of various shapes and sizes, tumbling out like lumps of coal in a hydraulic flush. Not constantly, but in sudden spurts after gurgling, sucking pauses. Two Chinese laborers wearing sack coats and thick mittens packed the ice into wooden barrels. Several dozen full barrels stood nearby.

Now and then the cabinet, or whatever the hell it was, emitted a sputtering, belching noise and shivered on its legs. But chunks of ice continued to spew out regularly enough to keep the industrious workers busy packing it.

"Jamie lad," Pinkerton announced with his usual air of melodrama, "meet Professor Albert

Vogel of Lubeck, Prussia. Meet also the magnum opus of his long career as an inventor: the refrigeration compressor."

Ice continued to bump and slither down the chute, mesmerizing Bill.

"As you can see, the professor's new compressor would easily fit into a train car," Pinkerton added. "Which it soon will. Yet it can produce . . . *how* much ice daily, Professor Vogel?"

"Nine to ten zousand pounds," the old man scolded, as if Pinkerton were a lazy student who had forgotten a key formula.

Bill blinked, staring at the old gent. "You misspoke, right, Professor? You don't mean five *tons* of ice? In one day?"

Vogel bristled, offended at being challenged by uneducated louts who toted guns. "Five tons, *ja*! In *one* day!"

"That's impossible," Bill said.

"Ach, not ven you have za inductive logic and za experiments! To be precise, it is *suction*."

As if in support of its creator, the cabinet shuddered and emitted a sucking noise like swirling eddies on a flooding river.

"Za main item required is suction," Vogel repeated. "Get you a wacuum started, and—*mirabile dictu!*—you have za refrigeration. Zen I had only to fill za outer pipes viz hydrogen and ammonia before sealing zem tight."

"A 'wacuum,'" Pinkerton chipped in helpfully, "is a vacuum."

"Thanks," Bill said dryly. "I never could have figured that one out without a real detective."

But watching all that clear, glittering ice tumble out like big sparkling gems put a dent in Bill's cynicism.

Pinkerton said, "I was bragging about how the death rate is way down this year at the fever pesthouse. Those barrels are why. Professor Vogel has been working night and day, without pay, to manufacture ice. I'm paying the workers myself. We're providing plenty of ice to artificially cool not only the worst-case fever victims, but the air in the sickrooms, too. And it's *working*, Bill! Some patients are even breaking their fever without any delirium or severe pain."

"I'll be damned," Bill said, admiration clear in his tone. "It's amazing, all right. But scientific wonders ain't my usual bailiwick, Al. What's my mix in all this?"

"Jamie, you spend too much time at frontier outposts. You can't truly appreciate the, ahh, controversies swirling back in the cities. But right now, artificial cooling, especially of people or the air in hospitals, is viewed with great disfavor in much of America. Puritan pressure and religious disapproval have hampered its development."

"*Ja, za schleps!*" Vogel cut in, spraying beads of saliva in his indignation. "A brave young doctor here in za States, he has modestly suggested ice be tried in just a few hospital rooms, merely for za test. He vass decried as Satan himself!"

"That's why," Pinkerton went on, "Professor Vogel's backers, who include some in the Tidewater Elite, have proposed this promotional train tour. It's the best way to popularize both the ice machine and the larger issue of refrigeration and—and—what do you call it, Professor?"

"Air-condizioning," Vogel supplied. "Zee artificial cooling of za air."

"The railroad is perfect," Pinkerton said, "since the public is still very excited by trains and anything to do with them. It's only been three years since Promontory."

Bill nodded. Pinkerton meant Promontory, Utah, where east had finally met west to complete America's greatest achievement to date—the transcontinental railroad.

"You still," Bill reminded Pinkerton, "haven't explained how I figure in."

"Ever heard of a man named Randolph Bodmer?"

Bill shook his head, still watching ice tumble out of the compressor.

"Bodmer has made his fortune down south in the harvesting, carriage, and storage of natural ice hauled from up north. But Bodmer knows about Professor Vogel's machine, and he also knows that ice machines will drive him—Bodmer—out of business quicker than a finger snap. So now Bodmer is champing at the bit to move from 'God's ice' to 'unnatural ice,' as its opponents call it."

"*Ja,*" Vogel cut in. "But ziss Bodmer, he is za greedy profiteer. I vant ice for *humanity* first!"

"Bodmer," Pinkerton told Bill, "has already approached the professor with a generous offer for the patent rights to the refrigeration compressor."

"I can take it from there," Bill said. "Since it's a familiar story, especially out west. This Bodmer gent is not one to be dissuaded by a simple no. So you want me as a bodyguard for the professor during his tour."

"A bodyguard and a *machine* guard," Pinkerton said. "The job pays five dollars a day, Jamie, and all living expenses are covered by the professor's backers."

"The pay's not bad," Bill conceded. "But I can do better gambling. And enjoy myself a helluva lot more. I don't like trains. Besides, playing nursemaid isn't my usual line of work, Al, you know that."

"As to enjoyment," Pinkerton said slyly, pulling a photograph out from the inner pocket of his tweed coat, "this tour is not your usual cattle run. It's being advertised as a luxury extravaganza, and the wealthy and famous are flocking to it. Bodmer himself has booked an entire Pullman for this tour. And he's bringing his fiancée along. A sweet young Spanish tidbit named Elena Vargas."

Bill took a cursory glance at the photo, then quickly snatched it from Pinkerton's hands to stare in surprised disbelief. He recognized the couple from the incident the day before at the Commerce Hotel. Bodmer's insolent eyes stared out, announcing to all the world that the fine-boned beauty on his arm was *his* property, bought and paid for.

Wild Bill grinned. He looked up and smiled at the professor, too, suddenly in a fine mood.

"The terms are just fine, Allan," he announced. "It will be a great honor to serve as one of Pinkerton's operatives."

Pinkerton shook his head. "You usually do the right thing, Jamie. But Lord knows, you do require your little . . . incentives. But do not foolishly underestimate the dangers here. Nursemaid? Pah, it will not be beer and skittles, laddiebuck! Bodmer is a resourceful man, and generally gets what he wants."

"Then *one* of us is going to have to gangway," Bill said, his eyes again cutting to Elena's mother-of-pearl skin. "Because *I* generally get what I want, too."

Chapter Five

"The toughest towns in the West?"

Bill repeated the question while he cleaned his Colts in the ruddy light of the new gas lamps in Josh's hotel room.

"Kid, a man definitely wants to fight shy of *all* of Johnson County, Wyoming. There's one bloody range war heating up between cattlemen and rustlers. I've also been out to the town of Tombstone in Cochise County, Arizona Territory. Every morning, you'll find a body or two in the streets."

Joshua Robinson watched Bill open the loading gate on one of his custom-order Colts and inspect the cylinders for damage.

"But among cowtowns," Bill went on, "Abilene was the first and still the toughest."

Josh sat at a little escritoire across the room from Bill, dipping a nib into a little pot of ink and blotting his sheets of writing with sand. He was putting the finishing touches on the first official dispatch he would file, first thing tomorrow morning from the Western Union office, as the far-west correspondent for the *New York Herald*.

It was a vivid description of Wild Bill Hickok's killing of Baylis. "A dispatch about a dispatching," as Bill had quipped. But Josh was swelling with pride, because he knew that most major newspapers in America would also pick up his story—a group of publishers had recently formed the Associated Press for the sharing of telegraphic dispatches.

"Got something for you here, kid," Bill said, quietly interrupting Josh's editing.

The youth looked up to see that Bill had crossed the room, carrying a worn leather saddlebag. He removed an ornately detailed handgun, swung the wheel out to make sure it was empty, then handed it to Josh.

"I've been carrying this since the war. Won it in a poker game from a Cavalry officer who claims he used it to wound Jeb Stuart himself. I believe the fellow, too. He's a Methodist minister."

"It's old," Josh said, not meaning it to sound like a criticism. The revolver was beautiful and even included a foldaway knife blade under the barrel. "*Thanks,* Wild Bill!" he added.

"It's French," Bill explained. "An old, but very well-maintained, LeFaucheux six-shot pinfire revolver. It's got one serious drawback. It takes pinfire cartridges, which go off too easy when you bump the weapon. That means *no* cartridge under the hammer until it's God-sure you mean to bust caps. Damnit, *don't* do that, kid!"

Bill snatched the weapon back from Josh after the youth cocked and fired it. "*Never* dry-fire any weapon, you simple shit! You could damage the firing pin."

Bill set the gun on a highboy near the window. "Right now I doubt if you could hit a bull in the butt with a banjo. So leave it out of sight until we can give you a few lessons with it. And don't say anything to that Quaker mother of yours. But *do* learn the workings of it. Get the feel of the gun's mechanism so you can break it down and assemble it in the dark. But no more dry firing, hear?"

"Yessir!"

Before he returned to his own guns, spread out on the end of the chenille bedspread, Bill glanced down to see what Josh was writing.

"What *is* this bunk, kid?" he demanded. " 'Wild Bill Hickok has plenty of acquaintances, but few friends.' "

"Well, it's true, isn't it?" Josh demanded.

"So what if it is? Some law against that?"

"Why . . .'course not, Wild Bill. But I mention it because most people have friends, is all, and I—"

" 'Most people' are less than one solid man, at least on the frontier. You scribblers worry too much about 'the public.' "

"I just—"

"Never mind, write whatever the hell you want to. I just chop wood, kid, and let the chips fall where they may."

Josh watched Bill return to his weapons. The youth wanted to pump Bill some more about this "promotional tour" that would begin the next morning. Josh had already read the itinerary Pinkerton had given Bill. From Denver, the first leg would be due east along the Kansas-Pacific Railroad to Kansas City, with stops at two Kansas towns where Wild Bill had worn a star: Hays City and Abilene. From Kansas City it was a short jog north to Omaha, then west again by Union-Pacific and Central-Pacific Railroads. The final terminus was San Francisco, with stops to include Ogallala, Nebraska; Cheyenne, Wyoming; and Salt Lake City, Utah.

But Josh had been trying Bill's patience all day long with questions. Now Bill would have to be coaxed out by increments.

"Wild Bill?"

"Yeah?" Bill ran a bore brush through one of his Peacemakers, frowning at an elusive dust speck.

"There might be certain hotel employees who like to meet with riffraff in the alley out back. And *maybe* money exchanges hands."

Bill glanced up. Josh shrugged, feigning innocence. " 'Course, I'm just a wet-behind-the-ears kid. Just like us greenhorns to *assume* someone has been selling your room number to reward-seeking scum."

Bill flashed a quick, sly grin. "I said you were green, not blind or stupid. But I'm still a step ahead of you, Longfellow. Why do you think we're passing time in your room—because I like the cathouse stink of your lilac hair tonic?"

Josh felt heat flood his face. "Ma packed that for me. Made me promise to use it. So I'm going double portions on it to get shut of it."

Bill's room was just overhead. Josh heard muffled sounds through the ceiling. He watched Bill check his watch.

"About five minutes," he predicted.

"Till what?" Josh demanded.

"Wait a spell, you'll see."

"I walked all over town today buying some new duds," Josh said. "Man alive, Bill! There's Help Wanted signs everywhere. But lots of 'em say 'orphans and bachelors preferred.' "

Bill nodded, squinting in concentration as he

placed a tiny drop of gun oil on the pivot screw. "A man can get rich out here in a hurry. But law hasn't yet caught up with commerce."

Bill glanced overhead as he said this last, checking his watch again.

Josh said, "What are you—?"

He never finished the question. A sudden, boom-cracking explosion rocked the building, knocking a Frederic Remington painting off the wall. A smile creased Bill's face as plaster dust settled and confused shouts filled the corridor outside.

"What in Sam Hill?" Josh said.

"C'mon, kid." Bill headed toward the door. "I'll show you why those signs call for bachelors and orphans."

Upstairs, Josh saw that a crowd had gathered around the door of Bill's room—or, more precisely, around the smoking hole where the door had been dynamited out of its frame. The interior of the room was a smoking shambles.

"I left the door unlocked and humped the covers up," Bill explained. "So it looked like somebody was sleeping."

"So that's why you moved your gear to my room," Josh said.

Bill nodded. "Now you see how it is, kid. You *still* want to go along on this tour with Wild Bill Hickok?"

Josh never hesitated. "Yessir! I didn't come out here to wash bricks."

"It's your funeral," Bill said. "Make out your will tonight, and write a letter to your ma. She sounds like a good woman. Make sure you tell her one last time how much you love her."

* * *

The next morning, just past sunup, Bill woke to an amazing sight: Young Joshua had transformed himself into a "frontier dude."

Or so the proudly beaming kid obviously thought. He was decked out in brand-spanking-new dyed buckskin trousers, a frilled rodeo shirt, a bright-red bandanna, stitched-calfskin boots, and gaudy, star-roweled spurs of Mexican silver.

Bill laughed so hard he rolled out of the bed and crashed to the floor, blankets sliding with him.

"If it ain't the Philadelphia Kid!" he sputtered between howls of mirth. "Tadpole, you're either a mail-order cowboy or a circus clown!"

Josh scowled. "Wha'd'you mean?"

"Christ! You own a horse?"

"No, but—"

"Can you even *ride* a horse?"

"Well, not so good yet, but—"

"Then what the hell you need with *spurs*? Kid, forget the dime novels. Sweat and glamour don't mix."

Bill pointed at the boots. "You're so green you wasted good money on farmer's boots without high heels. If you knew sic 'em about riding, you'd know that you need good heels to hold your feet in the stirrups. You *are* familiar with that word, 'stirrups'?"

Josh was bright red by now. Still rowelling him mercilessly, Bill quickly dressed. Then he took the humbled kid with him to the local livery barn where Bill had been boarding his horse, a pretty little strawberry roan named Fire-away.

"I want him grained every day and rubbed down good each night," Bill instructed the hostler, tipping him a half-eagle gold piece. To Josh he added:

"Don't forget. On the frontier, no better word can be spoken of a man than that he's careful of his horses. You ever do get a horse, go light with them spurs. Now, c'mon, Philadelphia Kid! Let's head to the train station and put our Montgomery-Ward cowboy on display!"

Chapter Six

Albert Vogel's backers had spared no expense in preparing a grand train for this special tour to promote the production of "artificial ice."

Two huge steam engines and a coal tender were followed by several fancy new Pullman cars to serve the wealthy. A string of third-class coaches would hold the less affluent passengers, for this was to be a democratic event. At Vogel's insistence, an extra caboose had been converted to house him and his refrigeration compressor. It had also been gaily festooned with floral garlands and red-white-and-blue bunting. On a bright banner bold letters proclaimed: ICE IS CIVILIZATION!

"Vogel's backers," Bill explained to Josh as they approached the crowded boarding platform, "are building a factory in Omaha right now to make more of these refriga-jiggers. The whole point of this dog and pony show is to drum up interest, and maybe a few orders."

Josh could hardly contain his excitement. "You know what that means? I'll be a sort of *science* reporter, too!"

"Christ, why not?" Bill said sarcastically as he cast an eye around in search of Pinkerton and Vogel. "Hell, you're a fully seasoned nineteen years of age. Been to grammar school too, I'd wager."

"High school, too," Josh added proudly, missing the sarcasm.

"Good God, strike a light! Call this boy Sir Oracle."

A train eased into town along the westbound spur, hissing to a steaming stop when the engineer vented his boilers. Josh watched as some of America's new "hobos"—impoverished and disillusioned Civil War veterans, mostly forgotten by their nation—leaped down from a boxcar. Bill headed them off and slipped each of the destitute men some tobacco and four bits for a bath and a meal.

"But, Bill," Josh said when the hobos had left. "That one was wearing Rebel gray."

"He's a veteran," Bill replied. "It's the battles and the blood that bind veterans, not the color of the tunic. Pound for pound, Johnny Reb was the best American soldier yet. Unless you count the Sioux."

A fancy fringed surrey pulled up, and Josh got his first glimpse of the lovely Elena since their brief encounter at the Commerce Hotel. Bodmer sat beside his pretty trophy with a look of possessive pride on his face. Neither of them had yet spotted Bill.

"Tilting hoops, gents!" a masculine voice in the crowd called out as Bodmer helped Elena down from the surrey—exposing a glimpse of snowy white calf when her whalebone crinoline tilted. This riveted male attention: Ladies' fashions, in the 1870s, boldly bared women's breasts yet modestly hid their legs. So most men were "leg starved" and lusted to see a bit of bare female limb just like *this*.

"Jamie lad!"

Josh spotted a distinguished older man in gray Burnsides and the new matching suit of the professional class. He was leading a frail but alert, even older gentleman across the platform toward them. Bill quickly introduced Pinkerton and Professor Vogel. The professor still seemed indifferent to the gun-toting Hickok, but he took an instant liking to Josh, despite his ridiculous "Western garb." He was especially happy to learn Josh was a journalist.

Pinkerton nodded toward the two hardcases following Bodmer and Elena, weighted down with suitcases and valises.

"The ticket agent got friendly after I slipped him a gold eagle. Those two plug-uglies are listed in the passenger manifest as Bodmer's 'domestic servants.' "

Bill snorted. "Un-huh. Oysters can walk upstairs, too, can't they? That white 'servant' has got a .44 double-action Colt tied low on his thigh. That 'breed's not only got himself a long-barreled Walker Colt, but I can see from here he's filed off the sight so it won't snag coming out of the holster. And you see that rifle sheath he's carrying? That's a Big Fifty Sharps. If those two are servants, Satan is their master."

Pinkerton nodded. "I liked your policy when you were the law in Abilene," he told Bill. "They stacked their guns when they entered town, collected them when they left. The railroads are afraid to prohibit weapons on their western routes, citing possible Indian attacks. I took that into consideration when I planned security for Professor Vogel's tour."

Bill was listening, but Josh saw his eyes taking in Elena. She purchased a sack of fresh fruit from a vendor, then selected a few penny-dreadful novels for reading during the journey.

"Comely lass," Pinkerton remarked.

"Hmm. The professor's machine loaded on board?" Bill asked, still watching Elena.

Pinkerton nodded. "Last night. And the caboose is double locked. That's where you'll be staying, by the way."

A vendor approached, and Josh set his carpetbag down to purchase a few roast-beef sandwiches wrapped in cheesecloth. Behind him, there was a racket and clatter of a conveyance braking to a halt. Josh heard Bill curse.

"*Yoo*-hoo! Wild Bill!"

Josh spun around and spotted Calamity Jane waving her Stetson at Bill from behind the dash of a rattletrap buckboard. Sideboards and a tarpaper roof had been added, forming a crude sleeping shelter. Bottles clinked from inside the shelter. Whitewash letters on the sideboards advertised DOYLE'S HOP BITTERS, "THE INVALID'S FRIEND AND HOPE."

Doyle's was one of the most popular patent medicines in the West. As a curative it was worthless, but its heavy dose of alcohol left the patients too drunk to notice.

"Howdy, Bill!" Jane sang out, blushing like a schoolgirl. "I heard you was in town."

"Well, God kiss me!" Bill muttered. He had been unable to duck. Now Josh watched him bite the bullet—he doffed his black, broad-

49

brimmed hat and said politely, "Jane. How are you?"

"Oh, fine, Bill, fine. A little lonely, is all. A gal could use some company. You know how the nights can be. By the bye, Wild Bill—did you receive my letters and poems?"

Wild Bill had faced the drawn gun of Baylis without flinching; now, however, Josh saw a little bead of sweat eke out from Bill's curly blond hairline.

"Jane, you know how it is. Sometimes mail is slow to catch up to a fellow out here."

By now, Josh saw, Calamity Jane's gravel-pitted voice had alerted everyone to the presence of Wild Bill Hickok. Bodmer, realizing Hickok was boarding the tour train, turned so red that Josh could almost whiff his rage.

Elena, in stark contrast, seemed quite amused by Hickok's awkward situation. But it was the "servant" Josh watched closest—the white man with the tie-down gun.

At first, before Jane's arrival, he had looked around constantly, like a man on the dodge. But now his speculative eyes never once left Wild Bill. The man set down his load and pulled out a sack of Bull Durham from his shirt pocket. Still watching Bill, he crimped a paper, shook some tobacco into it, and built himself a cigarette.

The other one, the hard-eyed half-breed, just smiled a sick little lopsided smile.

They know all about the reward, Josh thought. And they mean to collect it.

By now Bill had somehow managed to shake Calamity Jane. Josh saw Pinkerton grinning, Bill scowling.

" 'Poams'?" Pinkerton repeated, aping Jane's rude pronunciation. "You sly dog, Jamie. Is this a secret courtship?"

"Don't presume on your white hairs, Al. I've hit old men, too. Damnitall to hell, anyway! Somehow she's caught wind I'm with the tour. She didn't wander down here just by happen-chance."

Josh said, "Will she buy a ticket?"

Here Bill perked up a bit. "She can't, kid. She's banned from every railroad in the country. She gets drunk and shoots up the Pullman cars trying to start fights. No, she'll just follow along by the wagon roads. We'll be laying over plenty, traveling slow to demonstrate Professor Vogel's machine at the one-horse towns. She'll have plenty of time to be a thorn in my side."

"Your fault, Jamie," Pinkerton insisted. "You're too damned gallant to the woman."

"Gallant, my sweet aunt! The critter scares hell out of me. She's been to a palm reader in Old El Paso. That fool convinced her there's this, ahh, 'shared destiny' between her and me. God*damn* that palm reader! There's one I wish I *had* shot in cold blood, that ignorant bastard!"

A conductor in a tall shako hat hopped down onto the platform. "All aboard the Ice Train!" he called out to the milling passengers. "All aboard, please! Watch your step, ladies!"

Josh's eyes flicked again to the gunsel who had just built himself a smoke. Now the man's eyes cut from Bill to meet Josh's gaze, surprising the youth. The gunman struck a sulfur match on a front tooth and lit his cigarette.

Then his right hand went for his gun!

But before Josh could even cry out, the thug's

51

gun hand came up empty. He pointed his index finger at Josh like a gun muzzle, cocked his thumb like a hammer, then laughed as the boy's face flushed red.

Chapter Seven

"You're not *still* angry at me over our little tiff yesterday, are you?" Randolph Bodmer inquired of his fiancée.

Elena's dark, almond-shaped eyes looked away from her romance novel to coolly appraise Bodmer. " 'Our little tiff'? Isn't that a bit of an understatement? Have you forgotten you called me a whore?"

Bodmer, already in a foul mood after spotting Hickok a few hours earlier, cursed.

"Damn, honey! You hold a grudge until it hollers mama, don't you? I spoke in a moment of anger, for Christ's sake!"

"Yes, and for *Christ's* sake you will repent that moment for the rest of your life! No man calls me that horrid thing! I am a Vargas! My forebears advised Ferdinand and Isabella during Spain's Golden Age! Miguel de Cervantes himself wrote his great *Don Quixote* at our family villa in Seville. I am not some low fishwife you may abuse with coarse language, then coax into your vile bed."

Bodmer's lips formed a grim, straight, angry line. The couple rocked and swayed gently in one of George Pullman's elegant new railcars, which had gone into service only two years earlier. Carpeted floors and plush drapes kept

53

much of the dust and noise out. Gas lamps with crystal-clear globes were mounted in elegant brass sconces shaped like figures from ancient myth. Bodmer's private car even included a parlor organ for sing-alongs.

Outside, if one cared to lift the window shades and watch, the South Platte River valley gave way to rolling brown plains, an endless, treeless expanse of ground and sky.

"I've just about had a bellyful," Bodmer finally told Elena, "of your high-hatting ways! I don't really care if you're descended from Jesus Christ, and I don't set any stock in your weak-kneed religion. Add the great Vargas name to a nickel, and you'll have five cents, missy. Your old man is dead now, and *this* isn't Spain. I'm the only real friend you have. You best think real careful how things stand, hear me?"

"Or what, big man? You'll have one of your scurvy-ridden toughs kill me?"

But Bodmer was too angry now to continue the altercation without fists.

"There are worse things than death," he hinted darkly just before he stomped out of the car in search of Big Bat and the Dog Man. "And if I catch you so much as *looking* at Bill Hickok, you'll find out exactly what I mean!"

Bodmer kept a wary eye out for Hickok while he located his two toadies in the final third-class coach. No plush carpets, liquor closets, or private sleeping compartments here. Some of the passengers had purchased boards and cheap straw cushions back in Denver, and stretched them between the hard wooden benches. The air felt hot as molten glass and smelled of rancid sweat and grimy clothing.

"Welcome to the ash pit of hell," a disgruntled Big Bat Landry said, greeting his employer. "Sure you could spare the cost of our tickets?"

"Take the cob out of your ass," Bodmer snapped. He removed his hat to whack at flies with it. "I've got some good news. I'm rescinding my order about Hickok. Go ahead and kill the son of a bitch, and cash in on the reward with my blessing."

Dog Man, who was idly cleaning his fingernails with a match, flashed his bent-wire grin. "We intended to, boss, order or no. See, your pay can't touch ten thousand dollars."

"No. But I'll tell you fellows what. On top of what that rich Texan is offering, I'll toss in five thousand extra. I want Hickok cold as a wagon wheel! Speaking of Hickok, you two seen him lately?"

Both men shook their heads. "He's with Vogel somewhere," Landry said. "Either in the Pullman in front of yours, or in the extra caboose with the machine."

"Everywhere that old foreign fart goes," Dog Man tossed in, "Hickok shadows him. That skinny kid, too. The one dressed like a Cincinnati sissy, always scribbling down things."

Bodmer nodded, his sharp fox face concentrated in thought. "Don't make a play against Vogel too quick. The guests on this train include the lieutenant governor of Missouri and a first cousin of Cornelius Vanderbilt. Besides, Vogel's backers are powerful men, too, and they'll raise six sorts of hell if it's done obviously."

"Lot of ways to die out west," Big Bat said.

"True, my friend, but I'm making a finer point than that. I'm saying it *will* go to law if there's any proof carelessly left behind. You aren't back-shooting some greasy drifter at an end-of-track hovel. So let's just keep an eye on him at first, see how the wind sets. It must be done right, or we'll all dance on air."

While this conversation took place, an old man in frayed farming clothes, seated on the bench about ten or twelve feet away, out of earshot, was smoking cheap, foul-smelling Mexican tobacco in a corncob pipe.

"Christ, that stinks," Bodmer carped. He raised his voice: "Say, codger! Take that scent bag outside, it's bringing tears to my eyes!"

"Ain't none of my funeral," the old man retorted, turning his back on the trio.

Bodmer let it go. But Landry seemed to take it personally. He reached down and opened his poke, pulling out a tightly coiled "blacksnake" whip ending in a knotted popper. Big Bat gave a fancy shake like a Mexican dally-roper; the whip, like a living tentacle, instantly uncoiled itself. Bodmer watched, fascinated, as the West's greatest whip master deftly and effortlessly flipped his wrist. The knotted popper whistled through the air, caught the pipe, and ripped it from the old codger's toothless mouth.

"Good eye," Dog Man admired while the old-timer sputtered his indignant protest.

"That's a grand total of fifteen thousand dollars," Bodmer continued. "And if you look at it logically, boys, you need to kill Hickok *first*. With him sent under, Vogel will be a duck on a fence."

"Ice," Professor Albert Vogel explained enthusiastically while Josh scrawled notes, "iss za poor man's jewelry! In Paris during August, a bag of stale snow commands za price of a bottle of fine vine! *Ja!* But ice iss more pure zan snow, vich absorb za impurities . . ."

Vogel nattered on happily while Josh and Bill watched Hilda—Vogel's pet name for his remarkable refrigeration compressor—spew out more than enough glittering chunks of ice to supply the train's needs. Each Pullman had an ice closet, and Hilda had also supplied the kitchen, dining, and bar cars.

"Hilda's design iss sempiternal. Zat means she vill not quit, once za pipes are sealed and za suction created . . ."

Josh hung in there, while Bill seemed more interested in the caboose's security than in Vogel's enthusiastic spiel. The car was cramped, with the machine taking up nearly a third of the space. But the car was still fixed up fairly comfortably, with several bunks, a mirror and washstand, even a small woodstove with a tin-pipe chimney. It would be vulnerable from both doors, and clearly Bill did not like that.

Josh watched Bill glance overhead, his face thoughtful. Then Wild Bill checked the lock on the front door of the caboose and headed out onto the rear platform. Josh followed him out. They left the door open so Vogel was in clear view.

It was early afternoon, and Josh estimated they were about eighty miles east of Denver. And fairly flying along at twenty to twenty-five miles per hour.

Bill, keeping his back to the wind, slid a cheroot from his shirt pocket and bit off one square tip. He struck a match with his thumb, fighting the wind for a light and winning. He puffed the cigar to life. Then Bill handed Josh a quarter-eagle.

"I'm hoping to get up a poker game later, kid. Stop by the bar car when you get a chance, wouldja, pick me up a bottle of Old Taylor."

Josh nodded, pocketing the money. He still could not believe that he was actually standing beside Bill Hickok, watching his hero smoke and gaze out across the plains with those weathered, cold blue eyes that had seen several lifetimes of adventure already.

"Prime cattle country here," Bill said, nodding toward a vast herd visible on their left. "When I first came out here, after the war, you saw nothing but a few Longhorns that had strayed north from the Texas *Brasada* country. Now look—all these new Shorthorns and Herefords. Better meat that sells higher."

Bill glanced back inside, where Vogel was tinkering with Hilda's coolant mixture. "But it's all about to change," Bill added. "I hear some gent named Glidden has just patented a new fence line. Calls it barb wire. The big open ranges are about to get busted up into front and back yards."

"My editor," Josh said, "says history is about to turn the page on us."

Bill nodded. "I'd say he struck a lode."

Josh watched Bill grab hold of the iron ladder that led to the roof. He swung up onto the first rung.

"Where you going?" Josh demanded.

"Ease off, Longfellow, I'm starting to feel close-herded. I'm just taking a little peek topside. Keep an eye on Professor Freeze."

Blond curls rippling in the wind, Bill hauled himself to the top of the caboose. The moment his head cleared the top, he came eye-to-eye with a bearded, frowning giant.

"Why . . . it's Yellowstone!" Bill exclaimed.

"Cap'n Bill? Why, it *is* you!" roared out "Yellowstone Jack" McQuady as he reached one giant paw out to grab Bill's extended hand. "By the Lord Harry! So we meet again, sir! But not in no damned weevil-infested reb prison camp this time, eh?"

"I never thought we'd get out of Andersonville alive," Bill said.

"And you sentenced to die as a spy the very next day," Yellowstone added. "Fate took a hand that day."

Bill nodded. "That's when I became a poker player. So what is it, old campaigner? You hitching a ride?"

Yellowstone laughed, then shook his shaggy head. He had an ugly but affable face distinguished by an easy, snaggletoothed grin. Like many big men Bill had known, he had no chip on his shoulder.

Yellowstone nodded toward the iron wheel beside Bill's head.

"God help me, Cap'n Bill, but I'm a brakeman now! It's the clickity-click and clackety-clack for me, sir—the song of the rails! I'm a railroad man now, God bless my poor mother. 'My only lad, spared by the great war,' cries she, 'only to be killed by Union Pacific!' "

Bill nodded. Yellowstone's mother was not just being overly maternal. After switchmen, who coupled the cars together with metal pins while they were still moving, the brakeman's job was the most dangerous in the railroad business. Trains would not be equipped with air brakes for another decade, so they had to be stopped manually by brakemen, who ran along the roofs of the cars turning the brakewheels. Twelve hours on, twelve hours off, these brakemen lived on top of the trains, in sleet or sun. One false move could turn them into paste beneath iron wheels below.

"And you, Cap'n Bill?" Yellowstone demanded. He yanked down the beak of his pillow-tick cap. "What brings you to the famous Ice Train? Besides your trouble-seeking nature, I mean."

"I'm a Pinkerton man now," Bill answered, his tone that of a man confessing he had come down in the world a mite. "I'm keeping my eye on an old man, a machine, and a girl who's pretty as four aces."

Yellowstone nodded, tugging his chin whiskers and watching Bill with one butternut eye slyly cocked.

"I've read this 'n' that about Wild Bill Hickok. He's good to all women, they say. But he's got this special weakness for *quality* gals. Actresses and royalty and such. That's what I read, anyhow."

Bill shrugged, already backing down the ladder. "Life is too short to drink cheap whiskey, trooper."

"Smoke 'em if you got 'em!" Yellowstone roared back. "Cap'n Bill, you've got enough guts to fill a smokehouse. But you won't get old."

"My very point," Bill agreed. "By my own calculations, I've been dead three years already. But it's good to see *you* alive, Yellowstone! I'll

60

come back later, we'll broach a bottle to the old days."

"Wild Bill!" Josh shouted from below. "Hurry! We've got trouble!"

Chapter Eight

After Wild Bill had climbed topside, Josh had continued to interview Vogel about his amazing new ice machine. Already the professor had been forced to shut it down—the train was completely supplied with more ice than was needed.

Josh had been in the middle of a question when the knob on the locked door rattled. The young reporter glanced up sharply when it was rattled a second time. All train porters and conductors had been instructed to knock and identify themselves.

Vogel, an annoyed frown wrinkling his face, started toward the door. But Josh stopped him with a warning touch, shaking his head.

Josh recalled the virtual arsenal those two gunsels with Bodmer carried. Then the youth heard a noise that made his bowels go loose and heavy with fear: a metallic scraping sound as someone tried to pick the lock.

Josh leaped to the rear platform. "Wild Bill! Hurry! We've got trouble!"

Bill didn't bother climbing down—he simply let go of the ladder and landed hard on both feet, a gun in his right fist even as he landed. Josh pointed toward the locked door at the front of the caboose, and Bill nodded.

Josh watched Bill gently, but firmly, push Vogel into a side bunk, out of any potential line of fire. Josh's eyes cut to his carpetbag in one corner, but then he realized—feeling guilty at the relief—that even if he could fire the beautiful old pinfire revolver Bill gave him, he had no cartridges for it.

"Ease off, kid," Bill advised him. "You're here to write the news, not make it. Time may come when you have to throw lead, but don't rush it."

Bill holstered his Colt and plopped down at a little table that was bolted to the floor to keep it from sliding. He removed a deck of cards from his shirt pocket and began idly shuffling the deck.

"Open the door, Longfellow," he instructed Josh with quiet confidence. But Josh heard in his heart a great actor saying: *Let the play begin*.

He looked questioningly at Hickok, nervous about actually doing it. The little metal scraping sounds continued.

"Damnit, kid, don't be rude," Bill told him. "Let our guests inside."

Josh shrugged, turned the lock, and abruptly swung the door wide open, almost knocking one of Bodmer's thugs in the skull.

"*Jee*-zus!"

The white "domestic servant" with the perpetual sneer went tumbling backward, almost tripping Bodmer. They and the half-breed were crowded together on the crazily shifting platform between this extra caboose and the regular crew caboose, presently empty, just ahead.

Josh watched the white gunsel drop something and hastily scramble to pick it up—a bar key, a favorite tool of "cracksmen," or burglars, and safecrackers. It consisted of the shaft of an ordinary key fitted with several bits, for locks of the day were all quite similar in structure.

Bill ignored all of it, or seemed to. He riffled his cards and asked in a bored tone, "Something I can do for you gents?"

Josh watched Bodmer quickly regain his composure. Now the wealthy entrepreneur was staring at Vogel's refrigeration compressor— staring, Josh realized, with the same kind of lust men usually reserved for the right kind of woman. Professor Vogel, understanding that covetous gaze, quickly moved to block the view of Hilda. Vogel had already told Josh that Bodmer would have to look inside the machine, and the cooling mechanism, to steal anything useful.

"There's something you can *stop* doing, Hickok," Bodmer finally replied.

Bill cut the deck. "Do tell?"

Josh had to bite his lower lip to keep from snickering. The words Bill had just spoken might have been a yawn. And Bodmer didn't miss it.

"Yes, I *do* tell," he went on boldly. "I've seen the way you look at *my* fiancée. It's a good rule to check the brand before you drive another man's stock."

"Better take a closer look yourself," Bill said tonelessly. "That girl isn't wearing any brand. She's a maverick—free for the taking."

Josh watched Bodmer's eyes go smoky with rage. But he managed to reply coolly enough, "Free? I wouldn't put one red penny on that. Elena knows the better man."

"She will soon, perhaps," Bill deliberately

goaded him. "In a biblical sense, I mean."

Bodmer's veneer of cool composure now cracked completely. "Hickok, you're no god-damned hero. You're a cold-blooded killer."

Bill continued shuffling cards. "Opinions vary," he said reasonably. "I shoot first and ask questions later. Call it what you will. Maybe there's been some mistakes, maybe not. But my system has served me well, and I plan to stick with it."

Bill had their full attention now. He set the cards aside. His eyes cut to the heavily armed gunmen as he added, "Glad you fellows stopped by. I calculate I'll have to kill both of you before this trip's over. But I wanted to tell you that now so you can both live with the thought before I do it."

Josh gaped in astonishment. Even Bodmer, trying to look tough, was forced to laugh in nervous discomposure. His hirelings shot their boss lethal glances. Bill had made his chilling remark in the tone of a man soothing a fussing baby.

In the ensuing silence, no one knew where to look. Josh tasted coppery fear when the half-breed's right hand twitched closer to his holster.

"Do it," Bill said, and his simple invitation made the half-breed go pale and look away, his anger traded for fear.

Bodmer stood there in silent, impotent rage, stewing in his juices. Bill picked up his cards again, his face suddenly tired and his tone showing some irritation.

"Get out of here, all three of you. This is a private car. You've been warned. Next time you show in that doorway, I'll do the decent citizens a favor and skip the cost of trial and prison."

Josh saw Bodmer send a high sign to his dirt workers. They began to back off.

"Enjoy your little show, Hickok, you'll pay for this," Bodmer promised. "You can chisel that in granite. You *will* pay."

"That's cast-iron fact," the white thug tossed in. "Mr. Pretty Curls here has just bought the farm, bull and all."

"Don't let that door hit you where the good Lord split you," Bill called out just before Josh swung the door shut and locked it again.

"Vhat zis?" Vogel demanded, aiming a peeved glance at Wild Bill as if *he* had caused this barbaric episode. "You vild Americans haff turned my laboratory into za O.K. Corral! Ach, I am a scientist, I *must* haff peace and quiet!"

Vogel sputtered on, oblivious to anything but his important goal of transforming modern society through the new science of refrigeration.

"Kid," Bill said. "Go get me that bottle now, wouldja? I've got a hunch this is going to be a long night."

Professor Vogel, still muttering darkly about the hereditary imperfections of the American bloodline, curled up in his bunk and promptly fell asleep, wheezing like a leaky bellows.

"That old coot gets on his high horse," Bill remarked. "And he wouldn't last two days out here without nursemaids. But his heart's in the right place, and that machine of his is some pumpkins. Kid," Bill added, watching Josh deftly disassemble the firing-bolt group of the gun Bill had given him, "looks like you took my advice."

Josh nodded, pride evident in his gleaming, fresh-scrubbed features. "I can break the LeFaucheux down into its major groups, and reassemble it, in thirty seconds."

"That's under a good light," Bill qualified. "How fast can you do it in the dark?"

Josh looked up, trying to see if Bill was just playing with him again. He already admired Hickok greatly, but the man had a disconcerting tendency toward what Josh's pa, a judge back east, called "private irony"—it wasn't always clear when a fellow was supposed to laugh.

"I mean it, kid. You think guns only misfire under a gaslight? First time I ever had a stoppage in a shooting fight was in—"

"In 1865," Josh said eagerly. "In the public square at Springfield, Missouri. You killed Dave Tutt, a former fellow Union scout who had turned traitor and joined the Rebels."

"I was *going* to say," Bill cut in dryly, "*in the dark*. Jesus, Longfellow! Do you also know the names of the first team I drove for Overland?"

"No," Josh confessed. "But you really liked them. It was four big Cavalry sorrels, broke to the doubletree because they knew the old soldier trails so well."

Bill was stunned into a respectful silence. He poured another shot of bourbon, saluting the reporter.

"Kid, right now, when it comes to actually firing that weapon, you couldn't locate your own ass at high noon in a hall of mirrors. But we can fix that, and we'd best start pronto. Bodmer talks the he-bear talk, but he'll show the white feather if shooting starts. But not those old boys who were with him. Those two are hell-bent on throwing lead my—*our*—way. It's best to make sure you can toss some back."

"Starting when?" Josh pressed. "And where, Wild Bill? Besides, I've got no pinfire cartridges."

Bill glanced out the window. Brassy late-afternoon sunlight formed a shimmering haze over distant hills to the north. From here they looked like a pod of whales.

Bill, it seemed to Josh, was thinking out loud, not answering the question.

"Your ma's a Quaker," he said. "And though I poke fun at *thee* for it, it's a fine sect. I don't mean to go against a man's mother. But out here in the West, there's too many people like Bodmer, people who never learn. Out here it's a good idea to get handy with guns."

Bill's distant gaze focused squarely on Josh. "So no sense putting it off. Lay that pinfire down and take this."

Bill slid one of his pearl-gripped Colts from the holster, spun it so the grip was proffered, and handed it to Josh.

"C'mon out onto the platform," Bill said, heading out himself.

Josh followed, handling the .44 as if it were King Arthur's sword. He noticed a small brazing on the trigger guard.

"Bullet hit it," Bill said, seeing Josh look at the repair.

This could be the very gun that killed McCanles and his gang, Josh marveled. This could be—

"Damnit, kid, wake up, wouldja?" Bill snapped. "I'm not talking for my health. I said do you see that cottonwood down in the wash? The one with the lightning-split trunk?"

Josh nodded.

"Shoot the damned thing."

Josh thumbed the hammer back, lifted the heavy gun, began to aim.

"Don't waste time aiming," Bill ordered.

Josh looked at him, puzzled.

"Aiming is fine with a rifle," Bill said. "You just *point* a handgun. Like it's a natural extension of your finger. Point at your target and shoot, all one movement."

Bill took the gun from Josh. "Point at the tree with your finger."

Josh did.

"See how quick and easy you did that? So stop aiming. Kid, I don't just *draw* fast, drawing isn't the main mile. It's how fast you get the shot off that counts. Now, on my command, point this gun and shoot."

Not feeling very confident, Josh nonetheless did as he was told. At his very first shot, a fist-size chunk of gnarled bark chipped away from the tree.

"I *hit* it!" Josh said in a welter of excitement. "I *hit* it, Wild Bill!"

"Sure you did. Look who's teaching you."

Josh's first shooting lesson went on until the sun became a dull red ball on the western horizon.

When they were back inside the caboose, Bill said, "We can pick you up some pinfire cartridges in Kansas City, if not before. Meantime, you keep a weather eye out for trouble. Just remember, you're not strolling down Market

Street with your mother. And you aren't just *writing* about the Wild West now, kid, you've become part of the story. From here on out, your life is on the line."

Chapter Nine

"*Dogs*, but that man is purty!"

Calamity Jane took a few more seconds to study the handsome face of her beloved frontiersman. Then she loosed a tragic sigh and tucked the dog-eared photograph back into the Bible where she always carried it.

"Bill needs this Bible," Jane told her swaybacked team, for she talked to them all day long. "I'm a sinner, but I *believe*. Bill's just a sinner. Dear God, it's true Wild Bill's been scarce around the church house. But just think of all the scoundrels he has sent to Lucifer."

Jane lifted her homely, careworn face to study the country hereabouts. She had driven all day and all night. Now she was still in Colorado, but just west of Garden City on the Arkansas River in western Kansas. From here, the flat tableland near the river valley, she could see the vast plains undulating all around her like curtain folds. The westering sun forced her eyes to slits.

Jane had selected a spot where the railroad tracks, impeded by rocky bluffs, took enough turns to make a cow cross-eyed. The train would have to slow to a near crawl through this stretch. Jane had been able to get ahead of the Ice Train because it was scheduled for a day-long layover in La Junta, Colorado, site of the first demonstration of the ice machine.

"It's destiny, Bill Hickok," she said out loud. "Come hell or high water, the Lord means for me to be with you."

Jane gazed at a deep groove in her right palm—her "love line," that palmist in Old Mexico had assured her. The old visionary's third eye also confirmed what Jane felt in her heart of hearts. Her life was meant to intertwine with Bill's, like two separate but intimately close strands of a rope. Bill didn't realize it yet, was all.

Jane wore frayed men's trousers, an Indian-made beaded leather jerkin, and men's hobnailed boots. But she was still bursting with pride over the only clean thing she owned: her new "John B.," as everyone out west called John B. Stetson's top-quality felt hats, the first American plainsman's hat designed by an American for the American West. Annie Oakley, Jane's only female hero, wore a John B. Ever since Jane had seen her in Colonel Cody's show, she had wanted one.

But if Bill Hickok wanted Jane in a calico bonnet, by grab, she'd wear a calico bonnet! Not that Bill had so far shown much interest in whether she was even alive or not. Jane was used to such apathy from most men. Even on the woman-scarce frontier, where desperate men married "the first female off the train," Jane had received no offers of marriage.

Well, maybe she was no lady. But most of the "decent" people who boarded that train with Bill would stoop to robbing poor boxes. Jane had fled into the empty spaces to avoid the stupidity and greed of such people back in so-called civilization.

If only Wild Bill would share this solitude with her! But until such time as the Lord enlightened him, Jane was determined to protect Bill. That's why she had decided to sneak on board the Ice Train—to keep a closer eye on him. She had seen the heavily armed trash boarding that train, and she had seen how they looked at Wild Bill.

Jane found a thick, rain-sheltered covert near the river and stashed her buckboard there. The team she simply unhitched and turned out to graze in the hock-high bunchgrass. She might have to scour the countryside for them later, but they bore distinctive brands, and Jane had yet to meet a man—white or red—who had the gumption to steal horses from her.

For a few moments, her tasks done, Jane squatted on her ankles to smoke and finish off a bottle of Doyle's. She listened to the crackle of insects, the bubbling chuckle of the river, the soft song of the prairie wind. And she scowled as she recalled the beautiful Elena Vargas, whose name and striking face were in every far-west newspaper lately. Somehow Bill, a man whose reputation was carved out beyond the fringes of "high society," nonetheless always wangled a way to get near a beautiful woman.

Even hungover, Jane had no trouble shooting a plump rabbit at fifty yards. She skinned it and cooked it on a spit over a driftwood fire. By the time she had scattered the ashes, she heard it in the distance to the northwest: the *chuff-chuff-chuffa* of an approaching train.

Jane knocked the dottle out of her pipe and

moved closer to the stone bed of the tracks, where she hid behind a brushy knoll.

"Bill Hickok, you handsome bastard," she declared out loud, "you're worth a sight more to me than ten thousand dollars! God wants us together, Wild Bill, and you *need* my steady hand. Here I come, honey!"

All through the night, while Vogel slept like a dead man, Josh napped and woke, grabbing sleep in handfuls. Each time the young reporter's eyelids fluttered open, Wild Bill and some affable, bearded giant in a pillow-tick cap were bluffing each other over a hand of poker.

It was still pitch black outside when Josh gave up and rolled out of his bunk. Bill nodded toward a fresh pot of coffee on the little stove. He and the giant, bleary-eyed man were still playing cards.

"Yellowstone Jack," Bill said, nodding toward the sleepy youth, "meet Joshua Robinson, a newspaper fellow from the City of Brotherly Love. High-school graduate, too, by God! He could solve all the world's troubles, if only someone would hire him to write about them. All that, and he's fresh off ma's milk."

Josh flushed while the brakeman flashed a snaggletoothed grin. "Cap'n Bill's a son of a bitch, ain't he, pup?" Yellowstone said cheerfully, sorting out his discards. "He's been cheating all night long."

The Ice Train steamed into La Junta, in southeastern Colorado, near dawn and remained on a sidetrack all day long, drawing fair-size crowds to see the ice machine in action. The once sleepy little cattle town was currently booming, and no wonder. With prices for beef back east going sky-high, a modest herd of three thousand Longhorns might fetch a rancher $100,000—yet, he could drive the whole herd to the railhead here at La Junta for about a dollar a mile.

For the demonstration, the machine was placed on a loading dock under Vogel and Wild Bill's watchful eyes. The milling crowd included townies, cowboys, cattlemen, buyers for the feedlots, as well as local sheepmen and outlying homesteaders and miners lured in by all the fanfare.

Josh spotted Bodmer and Elena several times, venturing into town to frequent the cafés and shops. He also spotted Bodmer's two hirelings, skulking about the edges of the throng. But the onlookers included deputies and soldiers, too, and Bill and Vogel were safe, for the time being, in this crowd.

"You see how close Bodmer got to the ice machine earlier?" Josh asked Bill. "He even tried to peek inside while the professor was distracted."

Bill nodded. "We're coming between a dog and his meat. Bodmer made a mint from ice, but now he stands to lose everything if his competitors get that machine first."

"The professor told me," Josh said, "that man-made ice will bring the cost down to less than a tenth the cost of natural ice. But there'll be even more profit in it."

Professor Vogel had cheered up noticeably during the demonstrations. He seemed boistered by the crowd's oohs and aahs when glittering gems of ice tumbled improbably forth into the furnace heat of the hard-baked plains.

Free cocktails and soft drinks were provided, deliciously chilled with Hilda's ice. Vogel also demonstrated how emergency "ice beds" were being used to successfully save fever patients once given up as dead.

Josh and Wild Bill occupied ladderback chairs beside the humming and vibrating machine. Bill had pulled his hat low and was keeping his distinctive pearl-gripped Colts covered with his coattails to reduce the chance of being recognized. Even so, now and then a tongue-tied cowboy asked permission to touch him for luck.

"I've read every book Ned Buntline ever wrote about you," Josh said. "Does he tell the truth?"

Wild Bill mulled the question while his eyes stayed in easy motion, scanning the busy scene around them. "Ned Buntline" was the pen name of E. Z. C. Judson, a smart and cynical dime novelist and "promoter" who had made first Buffalo Bill Cody, then Wild Bill Hickok, a legend—and Judson himself wealthy.

"No," Bill finally admitted. "Mostly he lies. The mountain men call it 'tossing in another grizzly.' But nobody *wants* him to tell the truth, kid. Facing the truth is like staring right into the sun. So Ned 'shades' things a little for popular consumption."

"I won't do that," Josh swore.

"If youth but knew." Bill grinned, watching Bodmer emerge from the train, alone this time, and head toward the nearest saloon.

"I won't," Josh insisted again. "Even if my editor won't print it. I'll record the real truth for . . . why, for posterity, I suppose. Somebody will print it someday. Times will change."

"If youth but knew," Bill repeated, still tracking Bodmer's retreating figure. He stood and brushed cigar ashes off his clothing. "Look, kid. Stow the idealistic chin-wag and keep your eyes peeled for trouble. I'm going to stretch my legs a bit."

Elena was so furious and depressed that she had locked herself in her private sleeper for nearly an hour to cry into her pillow. How *dare* Randolph demand that she let him into her sleeper tonight! If she loved him, perhaps demands wouldn't even be necessary. Hers was a passionate Latin temperament, and she was unrestrained by the usual chaperones. But in this case, she thought, there would be more honor in selling her favors outright. At least then she would be an honest whore!

Now, hearing her fiancé exit the train in a huff, she quickly fixed her tear-streaked makeup and went back out into the privacy of the Pullman. Elena curled up on a cushioned sofa with one of her penny dreadfuls.

She was still trying to pick up the silly plot thread when someone tapped at the door behind her.

"Go away!" Elena called petulantly.

The visitor rudely disregarded her command and let himself inside. Elena's eyes widened and she put her book aside, sitting up. "You! But . . . but I said go away."

"And I will," the handsome man assured her. "Madam, I intend no disrespect. But your . . .

male companion paid an unwelcome visit to my car yesterday. I just wanted to return it."

Wild Bill Hickok touched the brim of his hat, smiled, then started to turn and leave.

"Perhaps your presence is not unwelcome to me," Elena said, surprising herself at her bold words.

A smile touched her visitor's thin, expressive lips. "May I ask you a question?" he said.

"Is it personal?"

"Very."

She flushed slightly, not expecting such candor. But curiosity led her on. "Yes? What is it?"

"I've read that the tight lacings on ladies' corsets kindle impure desires. Have you found that to be true?"

This time Elena flushed deeply to her very hair. But she met his mischievous eyes boldly.

"They crack the ribs," she replied. "They weaken the lungs, constrict the internal organs, impede circulation, and disrupt digestion. They sometimes make us swoon, too. However, I do not believe they inspire prurient interests."

"I'm sorry to learn that," Bill said, touching his hat again and turning to leave.

"However," her voice called out behind him just before Bill shut the door. "*You* certainly inspire them. Do stop by again, Mr. Hickok."

The dining car was located behind Bodmer's private car. Bill wove his way past white-jacketed waiters, who moved around cat-footed, balancing trays on their fingertips. Then Bill realized Bodmer was back, staring at him from the opposite end of the car—obviously trying to figure out if Bill had just come from seeing Elena.

"Did you enter my private car, Hickok?" Bodmer demanded when Bill reached him.

"Just came to see what's for dinner," Bill replied quietly. "Get out of my way."

Bodmer squared his shoulders, standing his ground. "Don't piss down my back and tell me it's raining, Hickok! *Did* you enter my car?"

"If and when I do, I won't have to pick the lock. Now, I won't say it again, Bodmer. Get out of my way."

Something in Hickok's tone sank through to Bodmer, and he did as ordered. But he called out to Bill's retreating back: "The worm will turn, Hickok! It's going to be a long tour. We'll see who gets the last laugh!"

Chapter Ten

Bill Hickok had learned, during his lonely vigils as a military scout, that a man never had to go without sleep. In fact, he was carrion bait without it. But the trick to staying alive was not to sleep too deeply.

It was just past midnight. Bearing due east now, the Ice Train was rolling through the grasslands of central Kansas. They had just crossed the all-important hundredth meridian, the official rainfall-demarcation line where the long grasses of the wetter East gave way to the short-grass prairie of the drier West.

Josh and Vogel were asleep in their bunks, lulled by the rocking caboose and the metronomic click-clack of the wheels on the tracks. Wild Bill, mistrustful of both doors, sat with his back to the south wall of the caboose. This left him with a clear view of—and a clear shot at— both doors.

Bill had dozed off some time earlier while playing five-card draw against himself. Now cards lay scattered on the table in front of him. But his confrontation earlier with Bodmer had left Bill primed for trouble. So now, to make sure he didn't sleep *too* well, the frontiersman employed a reliable trick he had invented years earlier while he was sheriff of Abilene.

Wild Bill's right hand, clutching a heavy bunch of keys borrowed from Vogel, dangled over a metal washbasin he had placed on the floor. As he settled deeper into sleep, Bill's fingers began to relax their hold on the keys.

Bill dreamed of high stakes and pretty women and friendly saloons. But soon all the cards in his dream had somehow ended up spattered with blood and scattered on a saloon floor. The rhythm of the train wheels began to whisper to him over and over with sinister clarity: *Aces 'n' eights, aces 'n' eights, aces 'n' eights.*

"What?"

The keys jangled hard as they fell into the washbasin, and Bill started awake, his face rigid with the focus of combat. A Colt filled his right hand even before he realized it was *his* voice that had just spoken that single, perplexed word.

But all seemed well. Both doors were still closed and securely locked. Vogel, sawing logs like a rusty crosscut blade, slept with one protective arm draped around Hilda's temperature gauge.

Bill's heart quit thudding so loudly in his ears. Still . . . he felt the cool tingling of his scalp that often preceded danger.

"You awake, kid?" Bill said in a low voice. But Joshua only muttered something incoherent, smacked his lips a few times, and resumed his steady breathing.

Bill yawned. He stretched the kinks out of his muscles, then poured a few more fingers of bourbon into his pony glass.

He cast his eye about for something to read. The first thing he spotted, poking out of Josh's new left boot, were the pages of the next dispatch the kid meant to file. He had fallen asleep working on it.

Knowing he shouldn't look, but too bored and curious not to, Bill pulled the pages out and let his eyes fall to one of the body paragraphs:

Wild Bill does not, like the mountain men who blazed the trails before him, despise civilization. He likes bourbon and gambling and women, among other amusements and comforts. But since youth Hickok has always been close friends with solitude. He has no deep need of human company or to sink roots in one place. He has always spent most of his time out beyond the settlements, always needful of pushing over the next ridge, always ducking the ultimate arrow.

"'The ultimate arrow,'" Bill repeated out loud, forgetting himself. "God kiss me! The kid is *better* than Buntline!"

Josh's sleepy voice abruptly surprised him. "You *really* think so, Wild Bill?"

"Sleep tight, kid," Bill assured him. "A man can't even *shovel* it this deep. You'll get on."

Soon Josh was asleep again. But Bill, wide awake now, drew each Colt in turn and palmed the wheel, checking his loads. He found himself wishing, once again, that Yellowstone was on duty nights instead of sound asleep right now in the crew caboose.

Bill had never had much patience with men who acted like superstitious squaws. Nonetheless, he couldn't shake that ominous dream voice from earlier: *Aces 'n' eights . . . aces 'n' eights . . . aces 'n' eights.*

Randolph Bodmer sat alone in his Pullman, drinking strong black coffee laced with whiskey and stewing over his earlier brush with Hickok. He started when a conductor poked his head in.

"Just a quick water stop, Mr. Bodmer," he explained. "We're at a little hamlet called Rushville. Be here about ten minutes."

Bodmer nodded and came to his feet instantly. It was well past midnight, and Elena had locked herself inside her sleeper hours earlier. Even before the train squealed to a stop, Bodmer leaped down and waited for Big Bat and Dog Man to join him in a smoke, as arranged earlier in La Junta.

"Got the ropes?" Bodmer demanded.

Big Bat nodded. A crewman was busy swinging a water hose into place to fill the train boilers from a storage tank mounted on tall stilts beside the tracks. Smoking and making small talk about the weather, the three men began strolling back toward the blue-black shadows at the rear of the train.

Despite the late hour, other men, too, had detrained to catch some fresh air and stretch their legs. Like different instruments tuning up, snatches of disparate conversations reached Bodmer's ears as he passed the various groups.

"—one hell'va gold strike up in Dakota territory," a portly businessman in vest and suspenders was explaining to several listeners. "The Homestead Mine is now the most productive gold mine in the Western Hemis—"

"—so the night before they drive the beeves to market," the next fellow, a richly tailored cattleman, was narrating, "they fed the entire herd massive amounts of salt. Next morning they watered the herd, just before weigh-in, and friends, those cows tipped the scales! They—"

"—was in *Harper's* magazine, my hand to Jesus! This doctor says the bathtub is a carrier of diseases, especially when filled with hot water and—"

"Why, who *is* he? Just the son of the Russian tsar, is all! Imagine it. Grand Duke Alexis Romanov will soon be touring the American West—"

"—read how this new Vaseline has become all the rage with cowboys. Those yahoos all keep a jar of it in their saddleba—"

Bodmer and his companions drew deeper into the silent shadows, even with the final caboose and well away from the other passengers.

"Stay below the windows," Bodmer warned them. "Work quick!"

While Bodmer kept watch, Big Bat pulled several short lengths of rope—tied into loops—from under his shirt. He tied these at key spots on the side of the caboose—located so that a man might grab hand-and footholds and reach the windows.

Meantime, the slim and lithe Dog Man had slipped into a cramped space between the wheel well and the frame of the caboose. With great care and discomfort, he could hug the axle housing.

"All ahh-bohh-*orrd*!" a conductor sang out from up front. Bodmer headed back toward his car, gravel crunching under his boots.

"Remember," Big Bat whispered to Dog Man, now tucked out of sight. "Vogel is small potatoes compared to Hickok. You heard that cocksure son of a bitch. He made his brag *to our faces* that he means to kill us. Let daylight into that bastard!"

The brief water stop, and Vogel's wheezing snores, roused Josh from his fitful sleep.

For the next hour or so, while the Ice Train steadily ate up the prairie, Bill sat with his head against the window and taught Josh the rudiments of survival poker. Josh noticed that Bill kept one of his cocked Peacemakers on the table.

"It's mostly water stops now, kid," Bill remarked at one point, tossing down a hole card. "But right after the war? Christ, trains had to make unscheduled stops all the time so the crews could cut down horse thieves vigilantes used to hang from the bridges."

However, Josh had happily noted that the "Wild West" was still alive and kicking. Each time the train passed through an especial notorious cowtown, for example, the brakemen were ordered to douse their running lamps—drunk cowboys loved to shoot them out. And once, men had to be recruited from the third-class coaches to help shovel grasshoppers off a stretch of track—the crushed mess was too slick for the iron wheels to gain a purchase.

Finally, sometime around 2 A.M., Josh felt his eyelids growing heavy. "A flush beats a straight," he muttered to himself. "And a full house beats a flush."

He returned to his bunk, still muttering.

"Don't let the bedbugs bite," Bill told him, riffling the deck. The last thing Josh saw, before tumbling over the threshold into sleep, was Wild Bill sitting there at the little table, his head resting against the window.

And behind Bill, the black-velvet fabric of night, its inky fathoms the color of death.

Dog Man could barely twitch a muscle for fear of tumbling off his precarious perch. But he could glimpse an opening above him. Now and then, when the tracks passed near water, trees abruptly crowded the railbed, and branches over Dog Man's head made cracks in the moon.

The half-breed bore his present discomfort with a stoic indifference. He had learned, while riding with Roman Nose in the days before the Indian Wars, to develop the endurance of a saddle horn. A man simply needed to close his eyes and visualize his suffering as a bright red ball. Then he only had to visualize putting that ball in a box outside of himself.

Thus Dog Man was able to wait a full hour before he carefully extricated himself from his perch. One groping hand found a loop of rope; he swung out, dangling like a mail sack, and cursed when his flailing legs failed at first to find another rope loop. But in a few more seconds, Dog Man was securely flattened against the south side of the swaying caboose, both feet jammed into loops like stirrups.

He just hung there a moment, getting his breath and unlimbering his cramped muscles. The confluence of the Smoky Hill and Republican rivers eased past. Dog Man glimpsed walls of sawed-off cottonwood logs—the big trading post that dealt with reservation Indians. In the ghostly moonlight, Dog Man could spot gleaming liquor bottles dotting the prairie as far as the eye could see in any direction.

Good whiskey . . . his share of the blood money for Hickok would buy plenty of top-shelf liquor.

That thought was like an elbow to the ribs, goading him on. The athletic Dog Man nimbly caught hold of the next rope loops and carefully eased his face close to the window.

His right hand slid the Walker Colt from its oiled holster. Dog Man's hard, flat eyes peeked inside. A moment later, strong white teeth flashed through his lopsided smile.

Hickok's blond curls were pressed against the window glass. He had been playing cards and evidently dozed off. It was all so easy that Dog Man felt almost disappointed as he slipped the leather thong off his hammer and thumbed it back. His finger curled around the trigger and began to take up the slack.

"Time to call in the cards, Hickok," he whispered. "You saw your last sunrise yesterday."

Dog Man's hammer was only a cat whisker away from releasing when his well-trained nose caught it: a very strong whiff of alcohol.

Confused, Dog Man glanced overhead just in time to glimpse a woman's homely face in the moonlight, staring down at him as if he were a snake in her baby's crib. Dog Man heard some lively cursing, saw the big outline of a Smith & Wesson, and leaped from his shaky perch even as the short-iron spat orange flame at him.

Chapter Eleven

"*Damn* you yellow-bellied egg-suckers!" Calamity Jane screamed as four grim-faced Kansas City constables bodily dragged her into a lockup wagon. "Ain't a man among you, you damned city squaws!"

Josh watched one of the constables go sprawling as the fighting wildcat managed to land a hobnail boot hard in his crotch.

"*Don't* hurt my war bonnet!" Jane roared out when her beloved Stetson flew off. "Bust my bones, not my conk cover!"

"By the Lord Harry," marveled Yellowstone Jack, watching Jane fight like a she-grizz. "No *wonder* you're hiding back there, Cap'n Bill! That ain't no woman, it's a Harpy loosed from hell."

Wild Bill was indeed "hiding," or at least hanging back near the caboose with Professor Vogel. The rest of the passengers on the Ice Train were still detraining at the huge Kansas City terminal.

"I talked to Caswell Jones," Yellowstone said. "Cas is one of the night brakemen. He saw somebody on top the cars last night, but thought it was no doubt a vet down on his luck. Him being a fellow veteran, Cas never enforces the railroad policy of no free riders. Nor do I.

But once the shot was fired, it forced him to report him—ahh, her, as it turned out—to the chief conductor."

"I just figured out," Wild Bill announced, "why she fired her gun. Look here, fellows."

Josh, Yellowstone, and the professor all stared at the rope loops still tied to the side of the caboose. Josh saw Wild Bill actually pale a bit when he spotted the last set of loops—right under the window where Bill had passed most of the night.

"Dammy, Cap'n Bill," Yellowstone said. "She's got a face like thirteen miles of bad road, and a smell to match. But looks like she saved your life."

Wild Bill nodded. His eyes cut to Josh. "Kid, have you seen that beady-eyed half-breed get off the train? Bodmer's 'servant'?"

Josh shook his head. For a moment, Bill grinned. "I don't see any blood. But if we're lucky, he's feeding worms somewhere back on the plains."

A few moments later, however, Josh saw Bill's grin melt like a snowflake on a river. Reality had just set in.

"Damn it all!" he cursed. "The woman saved my damn bacon! A man can't just walk away from that."

Bill fished several double-eagles out of his pocket and handed them to Josh.

"Kid, the K.C. jail is downtown in the court-house building on Division Street. Wait a bit. Then take this and pay Jane's fine. Even with it paid, they'll hold her a few days for disturbing the peace. Stop at a florist shop on the way and get her a nice bouquet, too, wouldja? Just sign the card 'Thanks from your friend, Wild Bill.' "

"Take a care, sir," Yellowstone warned. "You know this will only make her love flame burn brighter?"

"It can't be helped," Bill said crossly. "Looks like the woman saved my hide, damnit."

"Ach! Ziss is a vooman?" Professor Vogel, who had slept through the commotion the night before, harrumphed impatiently at all this foolish skulduggery. He loved the attention his ice-making machine was generating. But he had also come to the conclusion that Americans were little more than baboons who were permitted to vote. Just *look* at this vulgar, dangerous female! What else *could* you think about a race of people who threw eggshells into a perfectly good pot of coffee and covered their new floors and walls with tobacco spit so strong it killed flies? They were all insane!

"We'll be here for two days," Bill told Josh. "Then it's north to Omaha and back out west again. No gunplay is likely here in K.C. It's a law-and-order town. Their gun ordinance is strictly enforced—it's unlawful to carry or wear any firearm in a public place. Nor will they tolerate killings like Denver will."

Bill paused to nod in the direction of Randolph Bodmer. "But I can tell you right now: Soon enough, more lead *will* fly. Not only does Bodmer want to get at that machine, but I've ruffled his feathers one time too many."

Wild Bill looked disgusted, and Josh could guess why. For Bill, this "nurse-maid's" job was getting damned confining and boring. He couldn't get a decent poker game going, nor (despite her tempting proximity) could he do much more than enjoy the occasional flirtation with the beautiful Elena. But boring or no, this had not proved to be any featherbed assignment. Even on a moving train, a man couldn't put his back to a window.

"Hell's bells, Cap'n Bill!" Yellowstone interjected, reading Hickok's mind. "What have we sunk to, hey? In our day we drank Indian burner with the *best* of the mountain men, didn't we, sir? Bridger, Harris, Carson, Ogden, Fitzpatrick."

"The Sublettes," Bill chimed in.

"Christ yes, the Sublettes! We *raised* some hell, didn't we, chappie? Now look at us. I don't even own a horse no more, and no doubt you've forgot what yours looks like."

Vogel, tired of all this laymen's foolishness, mounted the steps of the caboose. He must prepare Hilda—soon train crewmen would again haul her out for more public demonstrations. Since security for the machine was critical, Bill, Vogel, and Josh would remain in the caboose while most of the passengers enjoyed luxury hotel rooms in the city.

Joshua set out on his mission to pay Jane's fine and deliver flowers to her. He also meant to stop by a Western Union office and file his latest dispatch. Man alive, but things were happening nineteen to the dozen now!

"Kid," Bill called out behind him. "Take some of that extra money and stop at Roundtree Brothers Gunshop on Seventh Street. Pick me up a hundred-count box of .44 shells. And get yourself a box of .38-caliber pinfire cartridges for that shooter I gave you. I got a feeling you'll be needing them before this trip is over."

*   *   *

Toward the end of the Ice Train's second day in Kansas City, Randolph Bodmer met with his paid dirt-workers at a smoky establishment called the Alibi Saloon. The three men shared an oilcloth-covered table in the back corner. The Dog Man, bruised and cut but otherwise undamaged, had stolen a farmer's nag and finally limped ingloriously into Kansas City only two hours before.

"You look like hell warmed over, chumley," Big Bat told Dog Man, pouring him a stiff belt.

"I damn near looked *dead*," the half-breed shot back. His tone made it clear he was in no joking mood. "Your foolproof plan," he told Bodmer, "didn't allow for a fool named Calamity Jane."

Bodmer, lost in a private, brooding silence, said little at first. The gnawing worm of jealousy cankered at him. Elena had gone off for the day, claiming to visit one of the city's thriving "hydros," for Austria's water-cure spas were currently all the rage in America.

But was she lying? Hickok's mocking words goaded like spurs in memory: *I won't have to pick the lock*. Was that overbearing bastard putting the horns on him right now?

"Hickok's clover is deep," Bodmer finally said again. "But it doesn't matter how lucky he is— luck comes in streaks, and streaks have to end. Boys, *I* go a great distance while most men are debating whether to start today or tomorrow. And I've fought too long, too *hard*, to get where I am today. I'm *damned* if I'll come a cropper over some old foreign fart with his nose stuck up a test tube!"

Big Bat, deprived of his side arms by city ordinance, had brought his beloved blacksnake whip along. He laid it on the table while he crimped a paper and licked it.

"You will so long as Hickok is alive," he reminded his boss calmly.

"I have a remarkable grasp for the obvious. We've *got* to stop doing this thing slapdash. Look at it logically. Hickok can't live in that damned caboose forever. Once we pull out tomorrow, I want both of you to watch him like cats on a rat. Find out his routine. We've *got* to find the chink in their armor and then pound away at it."

Bodmer showed them a front-page story in that day's *Kansas City Star*. The headline proclaimed: THE ICE AGE ARRIVES!

"Vogel's refrigeration compressor is catching on great guns. I hear this new factory in Omaha is already half finished. This could sink me, boys. We have to move full-bore now. My entire fortune is bound up in ice. And now, ironically, it's all *melting away* in front of my eyes."

"Speaking of chinks in Hickok's armor," Big Bat said. "Don't forget that snot-nosed whelp that follows him like a pet dog. Hickok may be a coy bastard, but that brat doesn't know his ass from his elbow. *He* may be the key to dousing Hickok's light."

"Good point," Bodmer said. "We'll watch him, too."

By the time the three men left the Alibi, Big Bat was drunk enough to be in a trouble-seeking mood. Bodmer watched for a hansom cab. Meantime, two hard-knit, dirty, bearded riders wearing butternut-dyed cloth trotted past on gaunt mules.

"Damned dirty jayhawkers," Big Bat said loudly. "Stink worse 'n pig shit!"

Both riders halted. Their greasy flop hats were burned and stained from doubling as pan holders.

"If you're feelin' froggy, mister," one of them said in his hillman's twang, "you jist go right ahead and *jump*."

"Jump *this*, you toothless sheep-humper!"

Quicker than a finger snap, the whip expert merely flexed his wrist, and the whip wrapped around the rider like a tentacle. One quick, hard tug, and he lay sprawled in the street, howling over a broken arm.

When the man's partner make the mistake of pulling out a ten-inch bowie knife, Landry roared like an enraged bull. His singing whip savagely lashed the knife man's face, ripping off a great strip of flesh. Again, again, and yet again the whip cracked. Big Bat, completely unaware now, continued lashing long after the second man, too, lay beaten in the street.

"*Landry!* Damnit, stop! STOP, Landry!"

Finally, with both Bodmer and Dog Man restraining him, Big Bat returned to his senses. The jayhawker lay moaning in the dirt, half skinned and unrecognizable as human.

"You goddamned fool!" Bodmer berated him as the three men ducked into a narrow alley between the Alibi and a hardware store. "This isn't Deadwood! You can't just kill a man and finish your supper in peace. Save it for Hickok, I'm telling you."

But later, when his anger passed, Bodmer secretly marveled at his hireling's display of brutal whipmanship. And once again he recalled that galling moment in Denver when Hickok's randy-stallion eyes had mesmerized Elena.

A bullet was too merciful for a woman-stealer like Hickok. He should be taken down a few pegs first—peg by painful peg. Bodmer crossed his fingers and placed his hopes on the whip.

Chapter Twelve

"There passes another Iron Horse," the Lakota Chief named Catch-the-Bear said bitterly. "Have you noticed a thing? Almost every time it goes by, we build a new death wickiup."

Catch-the-Bear and a shaman named Coyote Boy sat near the firepit outside the chief's lodge. It was too dark now to actually see the distant Iron Horse or its yellow-glowing eyes. But they could clearly hear it chuffing past, just south of the reservation boundary—an imaginary line white men forced red men to respect, or else.

"The hair-mouths brought this fever to our ranges," Coyote Boy replied. "And now Death rides on their Iron Horse."

"I have ears for this! Just as they have brought us their dripping disease, their devil water, and other 'marvels' to make our women into whores and our warriors into spineless drunkards. Even now, my only daughter lies wasting with the yellow vomit! So are dozens more. Hear the grandmothers even now, singing their sadness?"

It was true. The Lakota winter count would record this period as the Death Moons. Night and day now, the old clan matriarchs were chanting the ancient, minor-key notes of the cure songs—the same sad, monotonous rhythm once chanted when warriors used to ride proudly off to battle.

Death's powerful fetor hung over Catch-the-Bear's fever-ravaged village in the upper Niobrara River valley of northwestern Nebraska.

Catch-the-Bear's sad, almost liquid eyes gazed around the clan circles out of a seamed face that had seen fifty winters. Normally, this camp would look vastly different. The younger braves would be wrestling, gambling, and running footraces, the little ones playing at war or the hunt dance. But the men who weren't taken sick, or already dead, were staying quiet inside their clan lodges. Even laughter was discouraged amid so much death and sadness.

"The *Wasichus* have made women of us!" Catch-the-Bear stated. "A new hair-mouth law will soon take away even our hunting rifles! Nor will we even be permitted to wear our bone breastplates—these are for making war, the whiteskin headmen have declared."

Both men were silent, turning this problem over carefully to examine all of its facets. Even now, the wild flowers were ablaze on their ancestral hunting ranges. In the glorious days of freedom, before the hair-mouths and their "maps" and their lies, this would be the time to send out scouts in search of Uncle Pte, the buffalo.

Even now, their painted horses in the common corral were rested and in good fettle. But to what purpose? They, too, were no longer free to run on their own ranges. Now they spent their days stamping their hooves in irritation at pesky flies.

"*Hear* it?" the Chief demanded again, meaning the mournful cry of the steam whistle. In his present mood, the sound goaded him to a white-hot rage. "Not enough to kill us, they must *mock* us, too!"

"Earlier, I threw the bones," Coyote Boy announced. He meant the Pointing Bones, ritually tossed inside a magic circle to seek advice from the All Knowing Ones. "The high holy ones demand blood atonement."

Catch-the-Bear showed little in his face. He said only "Young Man Afraid of His Horses has told me this same thing. He is our last great chief now that Sitting Bull has fled north to the Land of the Grandmother Queen."

"And Young Man is right. The bones point west, toward the direction of death. The Day Makers are telling us: Only when Catch-the-Bear acts like a great Lakota war chief will this hair-face curse of the Yellow Vomit pass. *How* can we obediently stand and answer roll calls by those who kill our people?"

The chief's deep-set eyes looked out over this silent, ravaged camp. Finally he nodded.

"Before the *Wasichus* came upon us like locusts, then there were always two fires burning in my lodge. One for food, and one for friendship. But today, thanks to whiteskins, I must give my daughter a new name in hopes of fooling death! Now this place hears me when I say it, the friendship fire is no more."

Again they heard the mournful, retreating cry of the steam whistle. Both Indians finally met each other's gaze. The talking part of it was over; now came the hard doing.

"Blood atonement," Coyote Boy repeated. "I have heard a thing. There is a way, using tools stolen from the hair-faces, to tear up the road for their Iron Horse. The Mountain Ute, west of here, have done it, and so have white criminals. Young Man has these tools hidden in the sand-hill caves."

Catch-the-Bear was cautious here. All red men flat out refused to touch the talking wires of the telegraph—one could actually hear the big magic humming in these. But the tracks . . . why not? Desperate situations required desperate remedies.

Catch-the-Bear finally nodded. "As you say. Go round to the headmen and tell them we meet in war council in one full sleep. Meantime, the blooded warriors are to make ready their battle kits. We will all first cut short our hair to mourn our dead. And *then* we will paint our faces to avenge them!"

To Joshua Robinson's young, impressionable eyes, Omaha was a wide-open, raw-lumber, hurly-burly city with one obvious drawback, at least to a man with an untrained nose: the constant manure stench from the feedlots encircling the city. "The smell of money," locals proudly called it. But Josh had smelled finer perfumes.

From Omaha, the Ice Train bore west toward Ogallala, another major cattle-loading railhead of the era. Despite his excitement at the prospect, Josh secretly worried about one stretch of track after Ogallala—a forty-mile stretch that bordered the Sioux and Cheyenne reservations.

Common wisdom of the day held that Indians—even the once-great Plains warriors—

were no longer a real, organized threat. The widespread Army crackdown, following the humiliating shock of Little Bighorn, had ensured that. A bunch of ignorant, gut-eating savages had defeated West Point graduates, and this at a time when the new "professional soldiers" had plenty of critics in a land carved out by citizens' militias. Reprisals had been brutal. The red men, except for a few holdouts, were cowed.

But when Josh asked Wild Bill about all that, the frontiersman only watched him for a long moment with his calm and fathomless eyes. Then he replied simply, "Kid, the red man is a notional creature. It's always a good idea to watch your topknot in Indian country."

In Ogallala, however, they soon found more immediate concerns. Wild Bill, Yellowstone, and Josh were playing low-stakes poker in the caboose when a porter delivered a telegram from Pinkerton.

Bill read it silently, cursed, then read it out loud:

" 'Have just confirmed an ugly rumor. Half-breed traveling with Bodmer is in fact the gunslinger called Dog Man. Use appropriate caution.' "

"Is he fast?" Josh demanded. "I never heard of him."

"Faster than about thirty dead men," Wild Bill replied. "That's counting only the ones shot from the front. I'd say only John Wesley Hardin has killed more in gunfights."

"Hardin and you," Josh corrected him.

Bill ignored that truism. "Dog Man is doubly dangerous because he's not a boaster, and he never braces a man. That's why you don't know of him. He hides his light under a bushel, so to speak, and lures his victims into a death trap before they even realize it."

"Then it's good that I've wangled a shift trade with Cas Jones," Yellowstone said, tossing down his discards. "I've taken the twelve hours from supper to breakfast. Nobody's getting at your caboose from overhead, Cap'n Bill. Unless it's over *this* brakeman's dead body."

" 'Preciate it," Bill said. "Pinkerton will have a fit, but consider yourself on the payroll, Yellowstone. Jesus, kid! That's the second trick in a row you've taken! The hell have I created here?"

Josh, grinning proudly at his new prowess, scooped in his winnings. But he said, "Dog Man and the other one—Bodmer calls him Big Bat— are watching *me* all the time now."

Wild Bill nodded. It was Yellowstone who spoke up.

"*Course* they are. Even the Dog Man doesn't want to go toe-to-toe with Wild Bill Hickok. That bear at Raton Pass couldn't kill him, and the Rebels couldn't kill him, and even the entire goddamn McCanles gang couldn't send Wild Bill under. So they mean to kill him the easy way, if they can find one. You just cover your ampersand, tadpole."

"You best do the same," Bill warned the burly brakeman. "Bodmer is getting desperate by now."

Josh nearly leaped from his chair when someone knocked on the nearest door. But Bill never flinched. He had a gun to hand before Josh could take his next breath.

Hickok checked to make sure that Vogel,

busy cleaning Hilda's interior with an antiseptic solution, was well out of the line of fire. Bill tugged Yellowstone to one side.

"Who is it?" Bill called.

"Elena Vargas, Mr. Hickok!"

"Just Elena?"

"Of course! Who else? Are you *so* famous that a lady must shout through this door all day in hopes of seeing you?"

"Ach! Anozer vooman?" Vogel shook his hoary head, paling slightly. The memory of Calamity Jane still frightened him.

"If you'll excuse me, gents."

Bill kept his gun to hand, unlocked the door, and verified that Elena was alone on the swaying platform. Then he stepped out to join her, shutting the door on his gawking friends.

"To what do I owe this pleasure?" he inquired, his eyes sizing her up frankly from her pretty satin shoes to her magnificent silver tiara.

"I miss your presence," she replied just as frankly. "You stay holed up back here like a hermit crab."

"Maybe. You can thank your companion's choice in domestic servants for that."

"What do you mean?" she demanded. "He tells me nothing about his . . . business arrangements."

"I mean they're trying to kill me and Professor Vogel, that's what."

At first she bristled like a cat, the charge was so enormous. Then Elena's opal skin went pallid. She shook her head in confused disbelief. "No, you . . . I mean, Randolph is a strong-willed man, and very jealous, of course, but—"

"That's right, lady, he *is* jealous. You'll be in one mess of hurt if he catches you with me. So what are you doing here?"

"I . . . he *ordered* me to stay away from you. In the coarsest, most vulgar words imaginable. He even threatened me. No one talks to a Vargas that way!"

"Mmm. So you came back here to defy him?"

"Yes. And as I said—I miss seeing you."

She cast her eyes down modestly, ashamed for being so forward with him. Bill noticed how the long black lashes curved sweetly against her cheeks when she closed her eyes.

"Maybe you and I can have our little visit," he told her. "Personally, *I* don't care a jackstraw about Bodmer's blustering and threats. But you're another story. I believe he would hurt a woman. Tell me, does he mean anything to you?"

"Once he did," she replied bitterly. "I even thought I might love him. But that Randolph was a deliberate impostor. By the time I realized his true nature, it was too late. The banns have been announced, and I am bound by law."

Bill abruptly cupped her chin in one hand and kissed her on the mouth. "We'll see if it's too late. I don't think so."

"Be careful, Senor Hickok," she warned him when she could trust her voice again. "I am a Latin—you are a good kisser, and I have a short fuse."

Bill grinned. "Then next time I light it, I won't put it out. But for right now, you get on back to your Pullman, sweet love. Don't give Bodmer any reason to lash out at you."

She nodded reluctantly. "Those cuts on the

half-breed . . . and his disappearance near Kansas City. Are those two really trying to kill you?"

"You can take it to the bank."

"Then of course Randolph ordered it."

Bill nodded. "But listen. I didn't tell you all this so you can confront Bodmer. It's just a warning to a prideful girl. Take care, and don't provoke him anymore. From here on out, you let *me* do that."

Chapter Thirteen

Josh, using a stub of pencil, was making quick notes in his flip-back pad when Bill came back inside the crowded caboose, a mysterious little smile in his eyes.

"Stir your stumps, kid!" he called out heartily. "Brew us up some coffee, wouldja? Then run to the dining car and fetch us some grub. But keep a weather eye out for Bodmer and his gunthrowers. I'd feel better knowing where they are at all times. You can be our scout."

Sometimes it rankled at Josh, the way Wild Bill could order him around like he was a colonel's orderly. But he could tell now that Bill wasn't speaking figuratively—he was really trusting Joshua Robinson, an untested brat from the wilds of Olney Street, West Philadelphia, to give a good report.

A scout! Josh threw a handful of beans on to boil, then reported to the dining car and presented Vogel's letter of authorization from the sponsors of the tour. The staff were instructed to "ignore all expenses and make all amenities available."

Josh ordered ribs and potatoes and baked salmon, with plenty of French-custard ice cream and fruit sherbets for dessert. Vogel had read him the riot act, sputtering in bad English, when Josh once foolishly forgot dessert. The old eccentric ate a little, but indulged a powerful sweet tooth. And naturally he preferred treats made possible by Hilda's ice.

While he waited for a steward to prepare a huge tray, Josh glanced around the plush dining car. Though it was approaching sunset, it was still too early for a lively dinner crowd. There were only a few well-groomed men in evening coats and glossy paper collars, and a few fashionable ladies in bustles, boas, and pinned-up petticoats.

But Josh felt his pulse quicken when he spotted Randolph Bodmer's sharp features.

The businessman sat off by himself on a pleated-leather banquette along the south wall of the Pullman. There was no food before him, just a carafe of coffee and a folded newspaper. As usual, the self-absorbed Bodmer did not seem very eager to socialize with anyone around him.

He seems bored, Josh thought. Impatient even, the youth realized as Bodmer again thumbed back the cover of his watch to check the time. Yet he continued to sit there all by himself, pretending to read the paper.

Almost, Josh worried suddenly, as if he's making a point of being seen here. Maybe to construct an alibi later?

That last thought made Josh more eager to locate the whereabouts of Dog Man and Big Bat quickly.

"I'll be back for that tray," he promised the steward, and moments later Josh was on his way to check the third-class coaches.

He got lucky and spotted Bodmer's thugs

right away in the first smoke-filled, sweat-stinking car he checked. They both sat sweating on the floor, playing checkers, the board on a bench between them.

Moving slow and easy so they wouldn't spot him, Josh started to ease the door shut. A heart skip later, fire ripped into his right cheek, and Josh howled with surprise and pain.

Dog Man collapsed on the floor, laughing so hard he had to hold his ribs. Big Bat coiled his blacksnake up again and slid the whip back under the bench.

"Kiss for ya, squaw-boy!" Big Bat grinned through his red beard scruff. "You tell Papa Hickok *he's* gunna get plenty of them kisses himself."

Josh touched the swelling welt on his cheek. It was hardly serious, but it burned like hell.

Josh's Quaker leanings from his mother were tempered by his judge father's cast-iron sense of right and wrong. He also had his father's hair-trigger temper.

"You had no right to touch me, mister," Josh said in a nervous, but strong and determined, voice. "And the last man who hit me got drilled right through his goddamn heart by Wild Bill Hickok!"

Josh didn't even see the half-breed move. One second he was laid out on his back, laughing; the next, his long-barreled Colt Walker was out of its holster and pointed at the gaping reporter.

Despite his fear, Josh felt his jaw drop open in pure astonishment. That wasn't just honed reflexes—it had to be magic! There wasn't even a *blur*!

"Pups will bark like full-growed dogs," the

'breed told him. "But Hickok ain't here to carry your load. You best dust, dunghill, before I irrigate your guts."

While the others ate, Josh filled them in on Bodmer's whereabouts and the brief run-in with Dog Man and Big Bat.

"Something's on the spit," Bill agreed calmly when Josh fell silent. "Sounds like Bodmer wants to make sure his ass is covered. Professor? Why'n't you hand the kid a piece of ice for his cheek? Nice little war scar, Longfellow."

Bill lifted his coffee mug to his lips, then grimaced.

"Jesus!" he complained, scowling at Josh. "You could cut a plug off this coffee!"

"You said you like it strong, I—"

"Not strong enough to chew!"

"Well," Yellowstone Jack cut in, "I do hate to break up an important debate, but it's back to the traces for this old warhorse."

The brakeman stood, stretched out the kinks, then tugged on his pillow-tick cap. He snatched up his lantern and headed for the rear door of the caboose.

"Remember," Wild Bill called out behind his friend, "take care up there tonight. I'll stop by later with a bottle."

"And bring the cards," Yellowstone suggested. "Might be moonlight."

After the professor had dozed off, Josh and Bill stepped outside on the platform to cool themselves. It was baking hot tonight, and night heat was more suffocating.

Josh watched Wild Bill take a good look all

around them, including a glance into the crew caboose. His face looked brassy in the fading sunlight. Looking south over the vast, limitless, treeless expanse, Josh watched the wind move through the grass like waves. A nascent moon, white as bleached bones, appeared high in the indigo sky.

"Seems too peaceful to be so dangerous," Josh remarked.

"The mind," Bill said, "wants things to be one way or another. But it ain't that simple. Winning second place in a target match will win you a ribbon. But in a gunfight, second place is first loser."

" 'Second place is first loser,' " Josh repeated, and Bill laughed when the kid scrawled it down for his next story.

Soon they passed a deserted settlement, a cluster of sagging houses with weather-grayed boards. Now and then they also rolled past some homesteader's dugout, squat edifices of mud and lumber, their hind ends backed into the side of a hill.

"Warmer than any frame house in winter," Bill remarked of the dugouts. "Only trouble is, animals graze on your roof. I know a fellow who was crushed by his own cow up in Cherry County."

But Josh saw that, even while Bill made such small talk, his vigilant eyes left nothing alone.

"You think Bodmer's getting pretty mad, huh?" Josh coaxed.

"Mad? Christ, he's screaming blue murder."

Josh said, "Is Elena—"

"Stow it, kid. I don't discuss ladies with anyone, least of all news hawks."

Josh sulked, but Bill took no notice. Soon a cloudburst opened up, and for a few welcome minutes the rain came slapping down. When its hissing subsided, Josh said, "Bill?"

"Ahh?"

"How come you left Illinois in the first place? Buntline never mentions that."

"I had to," Bill replied tersely. "The law in Troy Grove was after me for stealing a steamboat."

Josh goggled in the new darkness. "Man alive! You stole a steamboat?"

"Sure," Bill said, poker-faced. "And damn near got away. But my big mistake was when I came back to steal the river."

Josh flushed at being so green. "Awww . . ."

"Fresh off the turnip wagon."

Bill chuckled softly as he slid a cheroot from his pocket. He nibbled off the end, tucked it into his mouth, struck a sulfur match with his thumb, and fired up the cheroot. Keeping the door slanted open so they could see Vogel, the two of them stood there in the rain-cooled air, watching their young nation roll past them in moonlit darkness.

Josh's young fancy was still stirred to fever pitch from his encounter earlier with Bodmer's hirelings. A war scar, Bill called his welt.

His mind was busy coining more adventurous notions when Josh felt something drop down the back of his neck. Just rain water, sure. But why so warm?

Josh touched the wetness, then looked at his fingers in the shaft of yellow light spilling through the open door behind him.

His thoughts scattered broad, and a liquid

fear chilled his veins—that was fresh blood on his fingers!

"Look, Wild Bill!" Josh showed him the blood.

"Christ Jesus," Bill muttered. "Yellowstone!"

He lunged at the metal rungs of the ladder beside them. "Kid! You bolted to the damn floor? Get your skinny ass back inside and lock the caboose! Break out your shooter and stand by. Ventilate *any*body who tries to force his way in!"

The first thing Wild Bill spotted as he cleared the top of the caboose was the lifeless body of Yellowstone Jack.

His surprised eyes, still wide open, stared unseeing toward heaven. The big brakeman's throat had been savagely slashed before he could even get his gun out of its holster. His pillow-tick cap lay beside him, sopping wet with blood. Bill looked at the former Union Army hero who had survived the carnage of Bull Run and Antietam Creek, the horrors of Andersonville Prison, only to die by a murderer's hand on the high plains.

But if he gave vent to emotions, Bill knew *he* was buzzard bait, too. The killer had to be nearby. Resorting to his usual detached alertness, Bill remained protectively crouched at the top of the ladder, trying not to skyline himself.

He quickly ascertained that no one was hiding on top the last caboose. *The rear door*, Bill thought, hauling himself the rest of the way up and stepping carefully over his dead companion. Bill already had a Peacemaker in his right fist.

Later, berating himself as a fool, Bill realized his stupid mistake. Still shaken over the discovery of Yellowstone, Hickok had forgotten his cardinal rule about covering his back trail at all times—he failed to first thoroughly search the top of the crew caboose behind him.

Only the sporadic shifting and swaying of the train saved him. Bill was hurrying along a narrow plank walkway, toward the ladder at the back of the last caboose, when a rough section of railbed below sent him stumbling hard.

At the very moment he pitched sideways, a gun barked behind Bill, and he felt a sharp tug as the bullet passed through the folds of his shirt under the left armpit.

By long necessity, Bill's reflexes were primed against back-shooters. Rather than recover from his stumble, Hickok let himself drop, even as a second bullet creased his back like a tongue of fire licking him.

Hickok tucked, rolled hard, and prayed he wouldn't run out of rolling room on the narrow railcar. The lithe frontiersman came up in a squatting position at the very edge of the roof, already fanning his hammer.

Coolly, deliberately, Bill shot the weapon out of Dog Man's hand.

"Pick it up, gunman," Hickok ordered him. "Then holster it. *Slow*. That's it, by the muzzle."

There was enough moon tonight for Bill to see that the half-breed was copiously sweating. But there was a bold, mocking tone to his words when Dog Man spoke.

"Best to shoot me now, yellow curls! That way you preserve the *legend* of your supposed man-

GET YOUR 4 FREE* BOOKS NOW— A VALUE OF BETWEEN $17 AND $20

Mail the Free* Books Certificate Today!

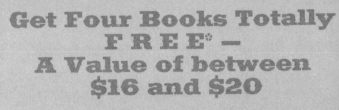

Get Four Books Totally FREE* – A Value of between $16 and $20

Tear here and mail your FREE* book card today!

PLEASE RUSH MY FOUR FREE* BOOKS TO ME RIGHT AWAY!

LeisureWestern Book Club
P.O. Box 6613
Edison, NJ 08818-6613

hood. No fool gives the Dog Man a second chance! I will piss on your grave!"

"Oh, I'll shoot you soon enough," Hickok promised calmly. "But the man who murders Yellowstone Jack deserves special. I mean to shoot you low in the belly so you bleed hard inside and die slow. I've seen it before. You'll lie helpless and screaming for hours, Dog Man, and you'll bleed so dry you'll *beg* for water. Oh, Christ Jesus, you'll beg! You'll burn up with hell-thirst at the end, and inside your belly? Why, like jagged glass churning—"

"Put a sock in it!" the half-breed snarled. At Bill's cold, methodical description Dog Man's face had lost its lopsided, mocking grin. His Colt Walker was holstered now. But Dog Man's nerves had become unstrung, and he hesitated.

"Satan's waiting," Hickok reminded him. "You came up here to get rich, you nickel-chasing son of a bitch. Now *earn* your blood money!"

"I said shut *up*!" Dog Man roared, and with the last shouted word he had his gun out and firing. But Hickok, true to his promise, had already planted two .44 slugs in the killer's intestines by the time Dog Man twitched off his first round, pulling it wide.

However, even as the half-breed tripped, rolled hard, then bounced screaming to the ground below, Bill realized a new source of danger.

He had been vaguely aware, during the tense showdown with Dog Man, that the train's angle had shifted as it headed downhill. Now that hill was steepening, the train's speed increasing.

Bill heard a desperate shout well out ahead,

saw a lantern wildly waving from the cars up front.

"Man the brake wheels!" a hoarse voice half commanded, half pleaded. "Hard turns now, Yellowstone, or we all cop it! *Now*, Jack, by the Virgin! You've picked a rum time to sleep— that's Crying Horse Canyon ahead!"

Obviously the front brakeman mistook Bill's form for Yellowstone's. Bill ran to the north edge of the roof, craned his neck out to stare ahead in the moonlight, then felt fear slam into him like a mule's kick.

The train was still picking up dangerous speed on the long downward slope. At the bottom, the tracks took a sharp, dogleg bend to avoid a steep canyon drop-off. And though Bill didn't know beans about manning brake wheels, even a soft-brain could see that the Ice Train, and all aboard it, were about to plummet to their destruction.

Chapter Fourteen

By now, Bill estimated, the out-of-control train was clipping along at forty miles per hour or better—dangerously fast, especially considering how long it took to stop even a slow train.

The front brakeman hopped desperately from car to car, cranking his assigned brake wheels until the iron train wheels below fairly screeched and shot sprays of yellow sparks up from the tracks. But his efforts were virtually useless with the rear half of the train shoving on ahead unabated. It was like trying to stop only the front half of a charging elephant. Nor could one brakeman possibly tend to all the cars.

Guessing the task by feel, Wild Bill grabbed the nearest brake wheel and turned it a spin or two to the right. When it showed resistance, he leaped to the next car and did the same. Bill thus continued to brake both cabooses and two of the passenger coaches—back and forth, back and forth, hustling desperately, turning each wheel as far as he could before leaping to the next and doing it over again.

During all this, Bill refused to look down each time he made the shaky leap between swaying cars. The train was definitely slowing, but had he braked it hard enough, and in time?

They slid into the dogleg bend, wheels screaming, sparks flying, and Bill felt the Ice Train lean dangerously to the north—literally teetering at the brim of the adjacent canyon.

God kiss me, we're going over, Bill thought. But then, before he could even leap to safety, the train came back to the level. Moments later, miraculously, it was through the turn and still on rails.

Bill heaved a huge sigh of relief even as the front brakeman loosed a wild cheer. His calves suddenly felt weak as water, and Bill abruptly sat down on the narrow plank walkway. He waited a couple of minutes to get his breath back.

"I'll face a gunfight *any* damn day," Bill said out loud to no one.

With the crisis over, the angry front brakeman was heading back to cuss hell out of Yellowstone Jack for falling asleep on duty. Bill stood up and returned to the top of the last caboose, waiting for the other man to arrive and learn the truth. It would take two of them, at least, to move Yellowstone Jack's body.

It was then, after managing to kill Dog Man and save the train, that the inexperienced Bill Hickok made the one unforgivable mistake of walking atop trains: He turned his back, for too long, to the direction of motion. Thus he failed to see the next turn ahead before he could brace his legs and lean into it.

The train lurched right, but momentum sent an unwary Hickok pitching headlong to the ground below.

* * *

In the Nebraska panhandle country one hundred miles west of the Ice Train's present position, the warriors of Catch-the-Bear's tribe had marked their faces with charcoal. Blackened faces symbolized joy at the death of an enemy.

"There! There is the signal fire!" called out the shaman named Coyote Boy.

He and Chief Catch-the-Bear shared a sandy knoll about thirty yards above the track bed. The evening bird chatter had fallen silent hours before. Below, in the ghostly moonlight, about a dozen sweating braves were ripping up the tracks with crowbars. These had been stolen from a *Wasichu* supply train headed for Fort Kearney. Indians knew how to employ them from observation of railroad repair crews.

"The next Iron Horse has passed Red Hawk's camp at Crooked Creek," Coyote Boy said. He was still watching the distant signal fire, an orange finger on the horizon.

"I have ears for this," Catch-the-Bear approved. "It will still be dark when they reach this spot. They will not see the missing rails in time."

The chief and Coyote Boy, like all the adult males in the tribe, had cropped short their much-esteemed locks to mourn the dead back in their fever-ravaged camp.

"We will kill and scalp as many as possible," Catch-the-Bear reiterated. "Remember, only the unborn are innocent! But we must also remember that most important is to escape with a live prisoner."

Coyote Boy nodded, understanding his chief perfectly. That prisoner would be tortured for days on end. Not only because torture was a time-honored tribal entertainment; this time it would also be an important offering to propitiate angry gods. Even now, Catch-the-Bear's delirious daughter, Mountain Laurel, clung to life by a bare thread. Two dozen more lay sick and dying.

"We failed to act like men when the gold-seeking hair-mouths first invaded our Paha-sapa," Catch-the-Bear added. He meant the Black Hills just to the north—the sacred center of the Sioux universe. "By that failure, we let the whiteskins bring their diseases to our ranges, to make women of us! But before our sister the sun is born again in the east, the Holy Ones will once again be proud of their Lakota *men!*"

The brakeman saw Bill topple off and shouted to the engineer to vent steam. So it wasn't long before the battered and dusty Wild Bill was back aboard the Ice Train, his usual slight limp now a bit more pronounced.

Josh watched Bill fill the washbasin and begin to unbutton his shirt.

"Nobody tried to get in here while you were up there," Josh told him. He added in a burst of candor, "Thank God."

Bill nodded. "That's because it wasn't part of the plan this time. They've been watching us. They knew I'd go topside sooner or later to jaw with Yellowstone. This move was meant to get *me* out of the way. The professor and his machine were next on the list."

"Once again Bodmer comes out clean as a whistle," Josh said angrily. "He's made sure he had a perfect alibi. He can blame the reward, claim greed made Dog Man act on his own."

"Won't matter," Bill said with quiet confidence as he quickly and efficiently shaved. "Alibis are for courtrooms. From here on out, *I'm* making the medicine and Bodmer is taking it."

"He won't give up," Josh said.

Bill slapped bay-rum tonic on his face. "No bout adoubt it, kid. You can see that in Bodmer's eyes. The arrogant son of a bitch senses doom for the first time in his life, all because of the professor's gizmo there. He'll foul his nest before too long. Bodmer's type always does."

"Bodmer!" Professor Vogel make a noise like spitting up a bad taste. "Ach, za prophet's eloquence, but za profiteer's honesty."

Vogel, who had previously shown indifference to the untutored Yellowstone Jack, had been shocked and outraged at the big American's brutal death. He had insisted on producing sufficient ice to keep the body in cold storage in the baggage car. And he had personally packed it all around the dead man, his eyes misty with compassionate tears. "He vass a brave man," Vogel explained apologetically. "He died protecting my Hilda."

Josh, his eyes big with excitement, watched Bill dry his hands, then remove each Colt in turn and check his loads.

"You're going after Bodmer and Landry, aren'cha?" Josh demanded.

"Kill one fly," Bill replied tersely, "kill a million."

"Good!"

Josh felt anger heat flow into his face as he recalled the way Bodmer had lately begun to insult and taunt Elena in front of others. That boorish behavior bothered Josh even more than Big Bat's stinging whip to his face.

"The way Bodmer treats Elena," Josh added, "is a sin to Moses."

Bill, carefully inspecting his firing pin for hairline cracks, gave a closemouthed smile. "What's the matter, kid? You been pining lately. You struck a spark for Bodmer's woman?"

Josh felt himself flushing deep. "She's *not* Bodmer's! She hates him!"

Bill looked up at him, and Josh suddenly regretted the insubordination in his tone. After all, who the hell was he, and just look who he was snapping at! But Wild Bill only shook his head, then holstered his side arms.

"Ahh, you'll do to take along, kid. Listen—break out your pencil, wouldja, and take down a note for me."

"Well, that just flat out does it," Randolph Bodmer announced when it was finally crystal clear the Dog Man was once again missing. "This time, I'll wager, we won't see him limping back alive."

Bodmer and Big Bat Landry had Bodmer's private Pullman car to themselves, Elena having once again sequestered herself inside her locked sleeper.

"He's dead," Big Bat agreed. "I searched the whole damn train except for Hickok's caboose."

Big Bat, his callused hands trembling, poured himself another shot of good rye. He was getting damned worried. Dog Man was a careful man, no risk taker he. He had ever followed the motto of his Mountain Ute clan: *Place no foot down until there is a rock to bear it*. And yet, even he had not been careful enough to face down Wild Bill Hickok.

Besides all that, the superstitious Big Bat had another reason to fret. Some old hag on the third-class coach had a cowl over one eye—a milky membrane that marked her as a visionary. Since she claimed to be an "astrological doctor," Big Bat paid her four bits to work up his chart.

She had concluded: "Your fate is in the Eighth House of the Zodiac." But the Eighth House, she informed him reluctantly when he pressed her, was Death's house.

Thus ruminating, Big Bat became aware that his boss, tongue well-oiled with liquor, was mixing personal matters in with business.

"—given Elena enough time to get over her little snit," Bodmer was confiding. "Hell, I never actually *called* the woman a whore, anyhow. Damned high-strung, fine-haired bitches! But instead of thawing out, she keeps giving me the frosty mitt! It's that bastard Hickok, he—"

Big Bat's ham-size fist slammed the table between them so hard that the whiskey bottle and glasses leaped.

"Get over your peeve, poncy man! Never mind your woman, they're *all* whores! Get your goddamn head screwed on straight, you hear me, Bodmer? It's us or Hickok now!"

Bodmer was shocked sober. Not a man to brook defiance, he couldn't believe Big Bat had spoken to him that way. But before the angry entrepreneur could even react, a porter knocked and entered with a note.

Big Bat watched his employer read it, then pale around the lips. Bodmer's eyes lost their focus, seeing something in his mind's eye that was inspired by the note.

"Well, what's it say?" Big Bat demanded.

Without a word, Bodmer slid the paper across to his hireling. There were only seven words, but they made the fine hairs on Landry's nape stiffen: *That's one down and two to go*.

But the note wasn't signed "Bill Hickok." The signature, in big, bold strokes of the pen, read: "Yellowstone Jack McQuady, Sergeant, Army of the Potomac."

Chapter Fifteen

It was in the still, silent, sleepy darkness just before dawn when the bottom suddenly dropped out of the world.

Or so it seemed to Josh only seconds after he was literally lifted and tossed from his bunk, crashing to rest on the now-tilted south wall of the caboose.

Vogel shrieked, probably because Hilda, too, had been tossed from her storage crate. She lay, apparently undamaged, against the wall beside Josh, trailing streamers of excelsior packing. Only Wild Bill, whose bunk protruded from the south wall, had not been tossed from bed.

For a long moment, right after the deafening, bone-shaking jolt, Josh felt everyone on board, himself included, hold their collective breath—as if in expectation. And sure enough, that expectant silence was broken by hideous, yipping shouts that frightened Josh immobile. Suddenly, things were happening ten ways a second.

"Son of a *bitch*," Bill cursed. "That's a Sioux war cry, gents. With the Crow or Cheyenne tribes, we might pay tribute and pass by. Not the Lakota! Get set for a hell-buster!"

Sioux! Josh had only seen Sioux braves in towns, and from safe distances, at that. But he knew plenty about them, and he knew damn well they were no tribe to fool with. However, he had no time to be scared—poor Professor Vogel was practically hysterical, and Josh worked to calm him. The old Prussian had already confided to Josh that he would rather be boiled in oil than scalped.

Shots opened up from outside, and somewhere Josh heard a woman scream. Was it Elena?

"Damnit, kid!" Bill snapped, kicking the glass out of the window near his bunk. "This is no time to give that old man a sugar tit! Break out your shooter and take up a position! We're under attack, you young fool, stop gawking like a ninny!"

Obviously the train had been derailed somehow. But Josh could see now, in the early light, that it had not been too serious here at the rear. Although they had been torqued off the rails by cars in front, they were canting at no more than a forty-five-degree angle, the caboose undamaged.

More shots erupted while Josh groped in the carpetbag for his revolver. Bill was still holding his fire, waiting for a sure target.

Josh scootched to the window opposite Bill. Despite the lightening sky, he could make out little at first.

"They're concentrating their attack on the front half of the train," Bill explained. "But Indians don't concentrate their fire very long before they move on to a new position. You'll see them soon enough. When you do, *don't* waste shots, Longfellow! Against Indians, taking out a horse is as good as the rider. And what did I tell you about how to shoot?"

Josh's mouth was so dry he could spit cotton. He swallowed a fear lump and replied, "Don't *aim*. Just point and shoot, like the gun was an extension of my finger."

"*There's* a feisty Quaker," Bill approved. "Good for thee!"

Josh spotted an orange streak in the corner of one eye.

"Wild Bill! They're shooting fire arrows!"

"Won't matter unless they land inside. The Pullmans have metal frames, and the wood on the other cars is coated thick with linseed oil to stop flames."

Vogel, convinced he was about to be scalped, crawled back into his bunk and huddled under the cover.

"There!" Josh exclaimed. "I saw one!"

In just moments, more mounted braves were visible in the grainy darkness. Some rode bareback on their painted ponies; others sat on flat buffalo-hide saddles. Josh glimpsed upraised rifles and stone war clubs. The hammering racket of their assault was unbelievable.

"Kid," Bill said sarcastically above the din, "I don't mean to spoil your first Indian attack. But don't you think maybe you better open the window or break that glass out first before you shoot?"

Josh felt heat in his face. "I was *going* to," he muttered defensively.

Bill's .44 bucked in his fist, bucked again. Spent cartridges rattled to the floor, and Josh whiffed the sharp scent of spent cordite. He groped for one of his boots to smash out the window.

A heartbeat later, an attacking brave did it for him. Shards of glass suddenly exploded inward when a double-bladed throwing hatchet destroyed the window.

"Man alive!"

Josh leaped backward as glass cut his face, the pain like dozens of fiery ant bites. But the blade missed Josh by an inch or so. The hatchet embedded itself hard in the wall just above Vogel's head. The old man screeched like a damned soul in torment.

"Let her rip!" Bill sang out, enjoying himself immensely.

But Josh failed to see the enjoyment—that hatchet had unstrung his nerves completely. He stared at it, snake-tranced, unable to move a muscle.

"Damnit, kid!" Wild Bill switched to his left Colt. "One useless old man per caboose is enough! Getcher thumb outta your sitter, Longfellow, and bust some caps!"

Much later, Elena realized it must have been all her pillows that saved her life—pillows imported from Paris and London and Canton, pillows thick with satin stitch and French knots.

The Ice Train had been traveling at about half speed—perhaps twenty miles per hour—when it plowed into the sabotaged stretch of tracks. The locomotive and tender had snapped free, ending up well away from the rest of the wrecked train. Elena's sleeper compartment, at one end of Bodmer's private car, was close enough to the front that she was thrown violently when the Pullman derailed.

But pillows cushioned that blow. And now they had also absorbed at least two bullets that might otherwise have found her wildly beating heart.

However, despite her good fortune, pillows couldn't cushion all the danger. The door to her sleeper had bent in its frame, and she wasn't strong enough to force it open. Even worse, when the Pullman tilted, gas lights shattered and set all the rich fabrics instantly ablaze. Elena was already coughing as acrid smoke filled the tiny room.

"Randolph!" she shouted desperately. "Randolph! Please help me, I'm trapped!"

Bodmer heard her, all right. But the snapping flames urged him to save his own hide. However, despite the lead ball of fear in his belly, the businessman couldn't help appreciating the poetic justice of this moment.

As far as he was concerned, Elena turned out to be nothing but money down the drainpipe. Why in hell should he chain himself, and his money, to a woman who refused a man the pleasures of the marital couch after all he had bought her? Since law wouldn't let him back out of a binding engagement, let fire or savages free him.

"*Please* help me!" Elena begged.

"Ain't *she* silky-satin?" he taunted through her blocked door. "Just too goddamn fine to touch, she is! Well, guess what? Where I come from, an empty hand is no lure for a hawk, m'love. You wouldn't come into *my* sleeper—why should I come into yours?"

127

"*Please*, Randolph, oh please! The smoke, it's choking me—help me—!"

"In a pig's ass, you snotty bitch! Let your famous 'Vargas pride' save you!"

Despite the terrible fear distorting Elena's pretty features, Bodmer's filthy and callous words filled her with loathing and contempt for him. She would beg no more—not from the likes of *him*.

Now the devout Catholic serenely sought shelter in her deep faith. As she often did in a crisis, she drew solace from the noble words of Perpetua, the Christian heroine who insisted on death by torture rather than renounce Jesus as her lord: "In the blood of the martyrs lie the seeds of the church!"

Thus resigned to death, Elena next came face-to-face with something even more frightening and unexpected.

There was a small ventilation window, barely big enough for a person to crawl through, just to her right. The glass abruptly shattered inward, and Elena was staring directly into a hideously distorted face covered with black stripes.

She was slow to move, but the battle-frenzied Sioux was not. Elena felt two strong hands like eagle talons seize her. She was halfway out the window before the terrified woman managed to scream.

Chapter Sixteen

"We won't be missed," explained the senior conductor, "until late today when we're due in Cheyenne."

"Then what happens?" Wild Bill demanded. He and Josh stood with a group of male passengers off to one side of the derailed train. The women and children had taken shelter in the two least-damaged coaches.

"The yardmaster in Cheyenne will telegraph Fort Robinson," the conductor replied. "The fort is about forty miles southeast of us. A search party will come looking for us. Course, they won't know exactly where to start."

Josh watched Bill nod as he mulled all this. It was well past sunup by now. Sparrow hawks circled in the empty sky. The men had just finished burying the engineer and fireman—both men had survived the crash but succumbed to Sioux arrows. No one else had been seriously hurt in the attack. Nor any prisoner taken except Elena Vargas. The Indians had taken their dead with them. But several dead ponies lay nearby.

"So you're saying that a search party," Bill said, "wouldn't likely get here for, say, two days at best? Maybe longer?"

The conductor nodded. "Two days is about

the same time it will take for number twenty-four out of Omaha to reach us from behind. That's the next train scheduled on this spur. We'll have to backtrack and leave a warning for them so they don't ram us."

Josh watched Bill consider whatever options they might have. A repair crew, made up of train crewmen and male volunteers, was already at work on the damaged tracks. But a service train from the Cheyenne railyard, equipped with hoists, would be needed to set the Ice Train back on rails.

Josh had noticed how the men, in the confused aftermath of the attack, had naturally turned to Hickok for leadership. All except Randolph Bodmer and Big Bat Landry. These two hung well back, sneering, but also very wary of Hickok. His note was still fresh in their minds. Not only was Landry armed to the teeth, he carried his deadly whip everywhere now.

Bodmer, Josh realized with contempt, couldn't care less about Elena's fate. Look at him, the bastard! Paring his fingernails like a rajah at his leisure.

"*We* can hold out two days with no real trouble," Bill said. "But Elena hasn't got a chance of surviving that long. Those braves didn't try to loot the train—nor were they painted and dressed for actual war. That means the whole point of the attack was probably big medicine. They need to get a prisoner."

"Why?" Josh asked.

"Knowing the Sioux and their grievances, especially since Iron Butt Custer, it probably means Elena will be sacrificed as blood atonement to their gods."

Bodmer, Josh noticed, continued to clip his nails and look bored.

"So what can we do?" spoke up Caswell Jones, the brakeman. "You want volunteers, count me in, Bill. That Miss Vargas is a little snooty, mebbe, but she's a quality lady."

At these words, Josh watched Bodmer say something privately to Landry. Both men snickered. Wild Bill, Josh saw, also noticed this. But he answered Cas in his quiet, businesslike manner.

"The usual way, in a hostage scrape with most tribes," replied the experienced frontier scout, "is to send a delegation to parley. But I don't think this is a hostage-for-ransom deal. So the usual way won't work."

Josh's belly growled loudly. His first set-to with real by-God savages had left him famished for a big plate of buckwheat cakes and hot soda biscuits smothered in sausage gravy. But he felt a stab of guilt for worrying about his belly while poor Elena was up against trouble something awful.

Bill tossed an arm around the shoulders of Josh and Cas Jones, easing them aside.

"Look," he said quietly, "this is the way of it. I'm caught between the sap and the bark. I've got to pick up that Sioux trail and scout ahead quick, or else Elena . . . well, you take my meaning. But I can't leave Vogel and his machine vulnerable, either."

Bill looked at the brakeman. "Cas, the kid here can hold his own with a barking iron. If you'll strap on a shooter and join him in the caboose while I'm gone, I'll see that you draw good wages for your trouble."

"Draw a cat's tail, Wild Bill. Any friend of Yellowstone Jack's, may he rest in peace, is a friend of mine. I'll join the lad gladly. But say! How will you scout without a horse, Bill? If that's Catch-the-Bear's bunch, their camp is a full day away on foot. With hard slogging in the sand hills. You ever *walk* in deep sand?"

"With any luck," Bill replied, nodding toward the west, "my providential horse is coming right now."

Josh glanced left. A slouch-hatted homesteader driving a big manure wagon was lumbering alongside the tracks toward them. In addition to the dray team pulling the wagon, an old gray plowing nag was tied by a lead line to the tailgate.

Josh watched the farmer's conveyance rattle to a stop when he slapped the reins over the backs of his team. The man was big-framed, but so skinny his backbone was rubbing his ribs. His face was tanned hickory-nut brown, and one of his suspender loops was unbuttoned.

Bill was about to greet the new arrival. Bodmer, however, had evidently decided to assert his undeniable authority. He stepped forward to greet the homesteader.

"Timely met, my good fellow! We're in a little trouble here."

"No misdoubting that," the man replied, and Bodmer frowned at his sarcastic tone.

"Keep a civil tongue in your head," Bodmer snapped. "How far is the closest settlement?"

Josh watched the weathered sodbuster gaze with undisguised contempt on this overdressed pack of city whippersnappers.

"Hell's right under your shoes, mister," he finally replied. "That close enough for you?"

Bodmer turned choleric with rage. Before he could sputter anything else, the homesteader added, his mouth set like a trap: "You can bawl like a bay steer, for aught I care. I don't let no son of a bitch talk down to me. Wheat's heading up, and the corn's well-tassled. I got better things to do than listen to your guff."

"Kid," Bill told Josh in a low voice, admiration clear in his tone. "You take a good look at that jasper. *That's* the backbone of America. A mild man until pushed, and then a hellcat unleashed. No more fear in him than a rifle."

The homesteader, having spoke his piece and spat into the dirt at Bodmer's feet, clucked to his team, about to move on. Wild Bill raised a hand to stop him.

"Never mind him, old roadster," Bill said evenly. "*I'm* the big bushway here. Mr. Bodmer there likes to talk loud to cover up his yellow spots."

The homesteader nodded. "Don't surprise me, mister. Mr. Bodmer is loud enough, all right. But 'pears to me he's got less get-up than a gourd vine."

Laughter rippled through the assembled men. Bodmer squared his shoulders as if in preparation for some action. "You setting up to be in charge here, Hickok?" he demanded.

"It's past setting up," Bill told him bluntly. "It's *set*. Now, shut your goddamn mouth or I'll kill you like I killed your murdering half-breed."

This did indeed shut Bodmer up. But not before Josh heard him mutter, "Don't worry, woman stealer, I been keeping accounts."

"Hickok!" the homesteader exclaimed. "Why,

so it is, there's the fancy pearl grips! My name is Junebug Clark of Zanesville, Ohio, Bill. I fought under Colonel Martinson with the Ohio Rifles—you scouted for my unit when our Negro recruits whipped the Rebs at Milliken's Bend. Touch you for luck, Wild Bill?"

Josh noticed a sea change in the farmer's manner. Clark informed Bill that there was no real settlement within a day's ride in any direction, just some stubborn and isolated homesteaders trying to prove up government land in rain-scarce grazing country.

Bill nodded toward the swaybacked nag tied to the wagon's tailgate. Its hips drooped with exhaustion. "That noble beast been broke to riders?"

"Maybe last century."

"How much to rent him for a bit?" Bill asked.

"It'll cost you one souvenir bullet from your gun—unfired," Clark hastened to add.

Bill nodded. Since fame had overtaken him, he gave away far more bullets than he fired.

Bill caught the eye of one of the stewards. "Knock up some grub for the trail, wouldja? Meat and bread."

Then Bill turned to Cas Jones and Josh. "While I'm gone, you two keep your noses to the wind. Bodmer is a bigger fool than God made him. And that Landry is shiftier than a creased buck. I'll be back quick as I can."

All morning long, while the sun inched higher and higher in a cloudless sky, Wild Bill bore north toward the Niobrara River.

If Bill hadn't felt so tired, he might have found

his present situation laughable. He had a fine little roan going to waste in a Denver livery; meantime, Bill found himself jostling along on a rough-gaited nag that was due to be sold for glue.

He had neither saddle nor bridle; no stirrups for his feet, no cantle for his tired back. Bill clung to rough mane and hung on with his knees, constantly coaxing the placid animal in the voice of a patient old friend.

Picking up sign of the war party had been easier than rolling off a log. The Indians had made no effort to hide their trail. For the first few hours, Bill actually enjoyed the hardships of being in the field again—he had practically been driven to "cabin fever," cooped up aboard the train so long. It felt good to remember how summer sun had *weight*, too, not just heat.

Soon, however, a dark thunderhead boiled up on the horizon. Before long it was pouring gray sheets of rain. There was no hope of cover in this open vastness, nor did Bill have a slicker. Scowling, soaked to the skin, he plodded on. Without a saddle, each jarring step of the plow horse was like a hammer to Bill's tailbone.

By early afternoon the sun blazed again, hotter than ever. Mud daubers were still active in the last puddles. Bill had finally worked his way out of the open, grassy flats into the hilly and forested tableland above the Niobrara River.

Bill let the gray take off the grass for a while as he, too, ate a meal and smoked a cheroot, resting. He figured the camp couldn't be much farther now. So tired his eyes were burning, he decided to sleep until evening, then move in closer for a reconnoiter.

135

When Bill's eyes eased open again, it was well after dark. Wild Bill felt rested and revived, and the evening air was soft as the breath of a young girl. A circle around the moon told him it would rain again before morning, but for now the weather was with him.

In less than an hour, Bill had reached a low bluff overlooking the clan circles of Catch-the-Bear's camp. As the hide tepee covers had aged, they had thinned like parchment, and now they let plenty of light through. With so many cooking fires going inside, cones of yellow-orange light dotted the camp.

Bill used his belt to hobble the gray. He left the animal grazing in a little hollow sheltered by boughs. Constantly sending his hearing out ahead of him, Bill moved in closer.

Here and there, in the light of a big clan fire, he glimpsed a clay-colored Indian. But the camp seemed oddly quiet—especially considering that a war party had just returned. But soon Bill understood why: With nightfall, the old grandmothers began their singsong chanting.

Cure songs, Bill realized. This was a fever camp. That explained the lack of the usual bustling activity one found in Indian camps by night. This camp, in contrast, was quiet as Boot Hill.

Bill soon located what must be the pest lodge—a big, temporary structure made from stretching hides over a bent-willow frame. And quickly enough, Bill also figured out where Elena must be—in that central tepee, in front of which sat several guards. At least she was still alive.

Bill made all these observations from behind a fallen tree. He had been careful to stay downwind of the camp, for Indians kept plenty of dogs around for security. All the dogs, and those guards, convinced Bill he could never slip in, free Elena, and slip back out. They'd both be killed.

But what could not be done by dint of sheer force *might* be accomplished by wit and wile.

The nucleus of a plan had formed in Bill's mind from the moment he realized this was a fever camp. It would be risky—especially in the first few critical minutes. But *risk* was Wild Bill Hickok's watchword. This plan would be a bold gamble, like staking it all on one poker hand.

What if you're dealt aces and eights? an inner voice warned him.

Bill made up his mind. He stood and unbuckled his guns, draping the leather gunbelt carefully from a tree limb.

For a moment, Bill wished he were pious so he could say a little prayer. Then, taking a deep breath to fortify himself, an unarmed Bill Hickok started boldly downhill toward the camp.

Chapter Seventeen

"I found a handy little spot about an hour north of here," Big Bat Landry told his employer. "Handy as a pocket in a shirt, matter of fact. It's an erosion gully in the sand hills. A man could hide in it easy, make him a little wallow. I could settle Hickok's hash for him and never show myself."

Randolph Bodmer liked the sound of this plan. He nodded his approval. Hickok had left hours earlier; now it was well after dark. The men were taking turns on sentry duty outside the derailed train—mostly just showing off for the women, Bodmer figured. The rest of the passengers had filed into the two least-damaged coaches at the rear. Bodmer and his lackey, however, chose to remain in Bodmer's severely tilting Pullman.

"If you mean to do it," Bodmer said, "you'd better take up your position soon. We can't know when Hickok might return."

Big Bat nodded. "Dog Man was a careful man, boss. But he still wasn't careful enough for Hickok. Me? I'm bound and goddamn determined to be *ready* for him."

Big Bat's present actions verified his boast: He had an arsenal arrayed before him in the guttering light of a candle. A weapon for any contingency: the dead Dog Man's scattergun for nighttime fights; the Sharps Fifty for distance shooting; his double-action .44 for close-in daylight fighting; a .38 derringer hideout gun to tuck up his sleeve; and a thin Spanish boot dagger when silence was desirable. And of course, his beloved blacksnake whip so's a man might have some *fun* while he earned his pay.

"What if Elena is with him?" Big Bat asked. "What do I do with her?"

"That's your concern," Bodmer replied coldly. "But I don't want to see her back here, you take my meaning?"

Big Bat grinned. "Don't worry. She won't come back. And she won't go to waste, neither. *I* don't mind eating off another man's plate."

"She's not mine," Bodmer insisted. "To quote Hickok: 'She's a free-range maverick. There for the taking.' Listen, have you seen Vogel or the kid since you got back?"

Big Bat, still busy inspecting weapons, shook his head. "They're not budging from the caboose."

"Well, we have to trot before we can canter. First we'll get Hickok out of the picture. By the time this train reaches San Francisco, Albert Vogel and that snot-nosed punk will join Hickok in the happy hunting grounds. And *I'm* going to have the design of that damned refrigeration compressor."

Faint heart never won fair lady. And a brazen man often outstrips the cautious one. Wild Bill discovered the truth of both old sayings as he walked closer and closer to the heart of the Sioux camp.

The dogs, which should have gone into a barking frenzy, either never caught wind of Bill or liked his scent. Soon, he was actually down among the circle of tepees. And several of the half-wild, half-starved mongrels had already licked his hand in welcome!

Bill crept up to the rear of the guarded tepee. He lifted the hide cover enough to peek inside.

There sat Elena near the center pole, unbound and apparently still unharmed. Her huge, dark eyes were water-galled from weeping, her complexion pale and opaque in the firelight. She had been taken from her sleeper before she could don the usual layers of petticoats and corsets. A thin blue anchor-print dress clung to the shapely curves of her body.

She reminded Bill of a pretty bouquet one day after the ball—still quite pretty, but starting to wilt. The look on her face said it all: What a viper she had taken to her bosom when she accepted Bodmer!

Wild Bill knew that a lodge erected by itself on a lone hummock must be the chief's. In Sioux camps, the chief was required to live outside the clan circles to symbolize his fairness to all. Bill dropped the tepee cover back into place and aimed straight toward this lodge.

But his luck finally ran out. He was perhaps thirty feet from the chief's entrance flap when a shout halted him. Within moments, Wild Bill was the hub in a wheel of scowling, well-armed braves that encircled him.

"Watallah!" shouted a warrior who held the stone tip of his lance at Bill's throat. He pointed at the long blond curls. *"Watallah!"* he shouted again—and Bill palavered enough Lakota dia-

lect to know they were calling him by the dead Custer's name: Yellow Hair.

One of the braves proved unable to abide this eerie similarity to the Lakota's worst enemy. Before Bill saw it coming, the brave slammed Hickok's head hard with the butt of a stolen Army carbine. Pain exploded in his skull, and Bill staggered. But he caught himself before he fell.

Knowing he was dead if he showed fear, Bill boldly spat in the brave's face. This show of defiance immediately impressed some of his captors. Now the famous gambler played his ace: He pulled a feather, dyed bright red, from his shirt pocket. He held it out so all could see it.

"Yellow Hair was a fool," Bill announced, combining Sioux and Cheyenne words, for the Lakota spoke both languages. Bill also knew sign talk, and signed with his hands when he couldn't find a word he needed. "Yellow Hair did not respect the red man or his might. *I* do. Do *I* demand that you grow gardens and wear shoes? Have *I* come into your camp bearing weapons, like Yellow Hair? No! I come to you in humility, unarmed, carrying only the *odjib*."

The *odjib* . . . the feather of friendship. In 1867, on a scouting mission for Generals Hancock and Sheridan in the Rosebud territory, Bill happened upon a dying Lakota subchief. The Indian's horse had tripped in a badger hole, leaving the brave stranded helpless with a broken leg.

Bill set the leg, fed the half-starved brave, and built a travois to haul him back to his camp. Hickok was rewarded with the feather of friendship, which declared the holder to be a true friend of the Sioux nation.

At sight of the *odjib*, the Indians did not lower their weapons. But a new uncertainty came into their faces. By now all the commotion had alerted an older brave, who approached from the direction of the pest lodge. Bill recognized him, from his feather-trimmed scalp cape, as Chief Catch-the-Bear. Not all those scalps, Bill noticed, were Indian—nor all male, either.

One of the braves spoke to his chief and showed him the dyed feather. Catch-the-Bear looked at Bill for a long time, his face as blank as windswept stone.

"Any spy for the bluecoats can color a feather red," the chief declared. "Why have you sneaked into our camp?"

"Sneaked? I walked in," Bill corrected him. "And notice a thing—how your dogs lick my hand. For *they* understand that I have come to save your dying people."

This dramatic announcement startled all. Clearly, the braves didn't know what to make of this.

"You are a shaman?" the chief demanded. "We have our own medicine man. Why would we want yours?"

"Indian big medicine cures *Indian* problems," Bill replied. "But only white man's medicine can cure white man's problems. And fever was brought to your ranges by the whiteskins."

There was undeniable logic here, and Catch-the-Bear only grunted. "Even if your hair-face magic *is* strong, why would you come to help us? You white men use Indian skulls to prop open the doors of your lodges! You go into our secret burial forests and rob the dead on their funeral scaffolds! Why help us now?"

"This is no mission of mercy," Bill admitted. "You took a woman from the train. I want her back. If you will give her to me unharmed, I promise to save some Indian lives. Perhaps not *all* of your sick. But I can save some."

Bill knew it was not the Indian way to haggle and dicker. A man simply stated his best offer first, and the Indian either took it or left it.

Clearly Catch-the-Bear wanted to take this one. But just as clearly, he was suspicious of such extraordinary claims.

"My daughter, Mountain Laurel, lies among the dying," he said. "This very night, we are set to begin testing"—Bill knew this actually meant torturing—"the prisoner. Her life for my daughter's! Can you save my people now? This night?"

Bill shook his head. "Not until tomorrow. Our medicine is a machine back on the train. If you agree, I will take one of your fastest horses and return this very night. We will bring it to your camp in a wagon. And *then* you will see big medicine, I swear it by the four directions."

"Meantime," Catch-the-Bear probed suspiciously, "the prisoner remains here?"

"Yes, but only if *you* promise not to hurt her, at least until I work my medicine."

Catch-the-Bear was no fool. The Holy Ones did not always work in direct, simple ways. What could this bold white man hope to gain from such a ruse, if that's what it was? No man need risk his life to steal a horse—the common corral was full of them. More likely, this sun-haired stranger was the agent of the Day Maker.

Finally, Catch-the-Bear's eyes regained their

focus as he returned to the present. He nodded.

"Come and eat something quickly," he said. "Then go cut out the pony of your choice. But I warn you now, whiteskin shaman—*hurry*. If my daughter goes under while you are gone, you will return to find your woman's brains bubbling over a fire. And *you* will join her."

Chapter Eighteen

"God*damn* it!" Big Bat Landry exploded.

The barrel-chested gunsel was so outraged that he heaved the Sharps Fifty rifle as far as he could, cursing again. It landed in the sand fifty yards away. The round in the chamber detonated upon·impact.

Damn that Hickok straight to hell! All night long, Big Bat had maintained his vigil in the erosion gully north of the derailed train. But despite his best efforts, he had dozed off at the first dull, leaden light of dawn.

And then, while he was still tumbling down the long tunnel into sleep, the rapid pounding of hooves had wakened him.

Even before he could curl his finger around the trigger, Hickok had raced past on a trim little black mustang with a roached mane. Far too quickly for Big Bat to tag Wild Bill.

Still cursing, Big Bat retrieved the Sharps and jacked another round into the chamber. Then he began the three-mile trudge back to the railroad tracks. To his east, the newborn sun was balanced like a brass coin just above the horizon.

When Big Bat's initial anger passed, a renewed determination took its place. He *would* kill that damned blond dandy, and he *would* be $15,000 richer for his risk.

"Your clover is deep, Hickok," Big Bat said out loud, quoting his boss. "But luck can't last a lifetime unless a man dies young."

"Landry is back now," Josh told Wild Bill. "But he went out last night, armed to the teeth."

"I was expecting to be dry-gulched," Bill admitted. "So I pushed that little cayuse like a bat out of hell. But never mind Landry for now—he'll get his comeuppance. Right now we best hustle—and mister, I mean quick. We don't get to that camp on time, it ain't just Elena in trouble—we'll *all* be doing the hurt dance. *Hep! Hep!*"

Bill, Josh, Professor Vogel, and Hilda the ice-making phenomenon were all crowded into a rickety buckboard, Bill driving. Junebug Clark's hardscrabble farm was located only a half hour's ride from the train. He had gladly loaned Wild Bill a conveyance and team—any effort to placate area Indians was fine by Junebug.

"Ach, *must* you go so fastly?" Professor Vogel demanded in his fractured English, almost toppling off the board seat when they jounced through a series of dry washes. "Hilda vill fall out!"

"Sorry, Professor," Bill replied, laying into the team with a whip. "But it's root hog or die now, so hang on, old-timer. Haw! *Hep! Hep!*"

Josh glanced nervously at the vast prairie behind them. It was all so big, a man lost his confidence for feeling so *little* in it.

"Landry will come back out here again," Josh told Bill.

Hickok nodded, his face half in shadow under the wide brim of his black hat. "He will for a fact. But like I said, kid: One world at a time. Landry can't kill me if the Sioux beat him to it."

Despite his fear and exhaustion, Josh was excited at the story prospects here. Ideas for a catchy lead paragraph were already popping in his brain like firecrackers. His editor might even increase his remittance payments after an exclusive about Wild Bill going right into a Sioux camp, bold as anything. Especially since Bill's dangerous mission was both a rescue attempt *and* a mission of mercy.

"Man alive!" Josh announced. "This is going to be front-page stuff!"

"That," Bill agreed, lashing the team again, "or a triple obituary. Haw, *gee* up there!"

Evening shadows seemed to hover over the camp by the time the three weary whiteskins arrived.

There was no time to rest or eat—two more fever victims had crossed over during the night. And Catch-the-Bear's daughter, Mountain Laurel, had entered the make-or-break crisis stage of her fever.

At first Josh could tell the Indians were clearly skeptical when Professor Vogel began filling Hilda's cooling chamber with water. But some time later, when the refrigeration compressor began to hum and rumble, awe replaced the skepticism in their faces.

But the true shock came when—smack in the middle of the hot moons of summer—*ice* began to slide down Hilda's chute!

Women and children, even a few stoic-faced warriors, fell to the ground at the sight of such magic. Indian shamans claimed they could work such miracles as turning enemy bullets into sand. But no one had ever produced such big magic as this before their very eyes.

Soon, however, led by the curious children, Indians were sucking on cool chunks of ice. Even so, Josh feared it would all be for nothing. For once Catch-the-Bear and the rest understood that Vogel actually intended to pack the fever victims—and nude, at that—in ice, anger replaced their awe.

"They mean to *kill* our people before our eyes!" insisted the shaman, Coyote Boy. He had been jealous of this magic all along, but too awed by Hilda to speak out. "Ice does not give back life—it *takes* life! Cold is not a good thing! How many of our people have frozen to death during the short white days?"

But Bill took Catch-the-Bear aside. He thumped the chief hard on the chest, Sioux style—a sign that the speaker's words came from a strong and honest heart.

"At least pre*tend* you have more brains than a rabbit," Bill goaded him. "If we kill your people, *we* will end up dead also. Even if you think we whiteskins are fools, are even *fools* eager to die hard?"

"You speak straight-arrow," the chief agreed. "Then work your medicine, Sun Hair. But do not forget what you said about dying hard."

Vogel drafted Indians to help. They used blankets and cooking kettles to carry ice inside the pest lodge. Eleven suffering Indians were moved to a shallow, ice-lined pit dug in the ground. A thin layer of boughs protected them from direct contact with the ice.

Once they were in the ice pit, more glittering chunks were packed over them on boughs. Once every fifteen minutes, under Vogel's constant supervision, each patient was pulled from the ice and briskly massaged to maintain blood flow.

As ice melted, Hilda faithfully replaced it, never once flagging. Toward morning, Vogel decided the patients had been refrigerated to the limits of bodily endurance.

"Let ziss last ice melt," Josh heard him say, pointing into the cooling pit. "Now zey are beyond za help of science."

Too weary to sustain their vigil any longer, Josh, Bill, and Vogel crawled into the back of the buckboard and slept like dead men until just after sunrise.

A strong hand shook Josh roughly awake. He sat up, thumbing crumbs of sleep from his eyes, to a gut-chilling sight: A dozen well-armed, stern-faced Lakota warriors circled the buckboard, staring in silence at the whiteskin outsiders.

"You came in among us making great noises, yellow curls," the chief said tonelessly to Wild Bill. "You spoke the strong-heart talk of the shaman. Now come, all of you. Come see the results of your tricks with solid water."

Josh couldn't interpret these expressionless faces. But the words sounded mighty damned ominous. Josh felt a cold fist grip his heart.

"It must not've worked, Bill," he said with quiet shock. "Aww, man, it must not've worked! We're—"

"Cinch your lips, kid," Bill snapped, still stretching out the kinks. "And stop looking like a nervous Nellie. Whatever happens, don't ever show fear around red men. They despise a squaw-man as much as they despise a liar."

Josh tried to do as ordered, but it wasn't easy. With a lance point probing his kidney, he marched across the central clearing. It had rained again during the night. Now the camp was so quiet, Josh could hear the trees drip.

The group paused in front of the elkskin entrance flap of the pest lodge. That fist around Josh's heart squeezed tighter. *Show no fear*, he willed himself. He copied the bored, slightly amused mien on Bill's face.

"See with your own eyes," Catch-the-Bear told them, "what your big magic has wrought."

Josh paused on the edge of his next breath. Catch-the-Bear threw the entrance flap back. Despite his best efforts, Josh almost had to sit down, his legs were suddenly so weak at what he saw inside.

"Wouldja look at that," Bill said quietly.

Josh gawped. Mountain Laurel lay propped up in her buffalo robes, hungrily sipping yarrow tea and smiling weakly at them! Josh counted six, seven—no, *eight*—more conscious, weakly smiling Indians.

Chief Catch-the Bear made the cutoff sign for the dead. Then he explained in a sad tone: "Two passed over to the Land of Ghosts during the night. And I have wept hard for them. But nine more, my little doe among them, were snatched from the jaws of death! May the High Holy Ones bless these three white shamans and their cold magic that gives warm life!"

Despite his relief, Josh was shocked by what the chief did next: He drew his steel knife from its sheath and cut deep into his own left arm, letting scarlet ribbons of blood run into the ground at his feet. But as Bill told Josh later—that dramatic wound was to ensure that the gods paid attention to Catch-the-Bear's oath.

"The girl," the chief added, "is free to leave with you. Go in peace, and may the Day Maker ride with you."

Chapter Nineteen

After speaking briefly with Elena, Josh and Wild Bill learned how Bodmer had deliberately left her to die a horrible death by fire aboard the train.

That tore it for Wild Bill.

"It was also Bodmer's direct order that got Yellowstone Jack killed," Bill said quietly to his friends. "Let's put the quietus on that murdering bastard."

So before the whiteskins departed Catch-the-Bear's camp, Bill requested another brief meeting with the chief. He explained who Bodmer was and the nature of his crimes.

"Chief," Bill suggested, "maybe your shaman had the right idea all along—I mean, about a hair-face sacrifice to your holy ones. Sure, your daughter has come sassy again. But what about protection against future adversity? This is no decent man—this is a murderer. *Any* tribe's God would welcome his death."

Catch-the-Bear nodded once. "I have ears. What is your plan?"

As Bill explained, even this stoic Sioux was forced to smile at the brilliance of Hickok's scheme. Bodmer's greed would literally become the death of him.

"It is justice," the chief agreed. "*Ipewa!* Good! We will do it."

Bill returned to his friends, now waiting in the tepee where Elena had once been a condemned prisoner.

"We'll fix Bodmer's wagon," Bill promised them. "But first I'll have to lock horns with Mr. Big Bat Landry. Here's how we're going to play it."

Bill had no intention of taking the others with him for the rendezvous with Big Bat. He explained that he was leaving alone, ahead of the rest, on Junebug Clark's old plow nag, which Bill had left grazing just south of the Lakota camp.

"Give me an hour," Bill told Josh. "Then you come along behind me in the buckboard. If all goes well, I'll be waiting for you to catch up with me after I take care of Landry. But whatever you do, *don't* return to the train with the machine or the buckboard."

Josh frowned. "What do we do with them?"

Bill grinned. "Give me your pencil, Longfellow, and a scrap of paper."

Bill quickly drew an accurate sketch map of the area—his years as an Army scout had left Wild Bill an excellent "minute cartographer."

"Three miles north of the tracks," Bill explained, "there's this little stock pond to the right of the trail we took. There's a thick stand of cottonwoods and a screen of buffaloberry bushes. You and Elena leave the buckboard, the machine, and the professor hidden there. You two will walk back to the tracks."

Josh cast a shy, sidelong glance at Elena.

Three miles all alone with her! Bill's plan was fine by Josh. But not by Vogel.

"Ach," he protested. "You vill leave me in ziss ugly dessert?"

"Just hold your taters, Professor. I figured you'd insist on staying with Hilda," Bill said.

"*Ja,* of course! Ver she go, *I* go."

"You'll be safe," Bill promised. "Just watch out for snakes. The Sioux are in on this with us."

"I trust you," Elena told Bill. "But will *you* be safe?"

Bill grinned. "I'll be safe, pretty lady, when I'm dead."

Bill looked at Josh again. "Now listen, kid," he added, "here's your story when you return to the train. . . ."

It was late afternoon, a westering sun throwing long, flat shadows toward the east, when Wild Bill finally reached the sand hill country of the northern Nebraska panhandle.

This stretch was where the ambush would come—Bill was sure of it. Just as those sand hills were the haven of cattle rustlers with running irons, they would also accommodate a dry-gulcher like Landry.

Patiently, Bill urged the old gray onward, his eyes constantly scanning the terrain. The thongs were off his hammers, and each cocked Colt held six beans in the wheel. Now, the readiness was all. . . .

One thing that had helped save Bill's life for years now was all the uncertainty as to his real whereabouts. Rumors about his supposed locations were always thicker than toads after a hard rain. But that advantage was gone now—Landry knew where to find him.

Something rustled to his left, and Bill had a Peacemaker to hand in an eyeblink. But it was only a badger crawling into its hole.

Wild Bill was still holstering his Colt after this false alarm when a stinging, smashing blow across his face suddenly blinded him.

But it was much more than a hard blow. Even as Bill sucked in a hissing breath at the pain, he was literally tugged off the gray. He smashed into the sand hard on his right shoulder.

Only now, as more swift, hot lashes of pain stripped the skin from him, did Bill understand that a whip had pulled him to the ground.

Hickok had tasted his share of whip lashings. But this was no typical cowhiding. Even as Bill groped for his right-hand Colt, the assailant expertly used the knotted popper of the whip to flick the weapon out of his holster. Bill's .44 spun fifteen feet away into the sand.

He rolled onto his right hip, drew his left-hand gun, and felt it too lashed from his hand.

"A fish always looks bigger underwater, Hickok!" Landry's voice taunted him. "You ain't so damn big *now*, are you, fancy man?"

Landry had to say all this between heaving breaths, because he was so vigorously thrashing his victim. Again and again his blacksnake whip whistled and cracked. Each time, the knotted leather ripped Bill's skin open, exposing strips of raw, stinging flesh.

"I'm a rich toff now, Hickok! It ain't just the pleasure of snuffing out your candle, you perfumed lapdog! I'm takin' your head down to

155

Texas and cashing in! Chew on *that*, lover boy!"

By now, Bill's shirt and rawhide vest were tattered, blood-soaked streamers. Each blow sent more blood spattering to the sand; Bill's last coherent thought was that he would bleed to death if he couldn't stop this lethal madman *now*.

"The *big* man!" Landry taunted. " 'Touch you for luck, Wild Bill?' *Shit!* I'll 'touch' you, you pretty little prissy. I'll—"

Wild Bill had faced death too many times to take it lying down. As the next stinging whiplash landed on him, Bill suddenly went on the offensive. Despite the hot flaring of pain in his limbs, he grabbed hold of the popper and tugged it with every ounce of will and muscle left in him.

Big Bat, his grip on the whip secure, had not expected such a move. He made the mistake of not letting go in time. He lost his footing, stumbled forward hard, crashed heavily into the sand. And before the big, clumsy man could move, the lighter and more athletic Bill was on him with the ferocity of a wolverine.

Hickok's lacerated body was not up to a wrestling match. Nor could Bill hope, in his present condition, to outslug this brick outhouse of a man. In a smooth "dally-roping" move that would have made a Texas cowhand proud, Bill wrapped the popper of the whip around Landry's neck and started squeezing.

The big man fought death hard. Bill, every nerve ending in his body feeling raw and exposed, rode him like a bucking bronc, refusing to let up.

"Next stop is hell," Bill goaded the gunsel.

"And it's going to be a long layover!"

Landry's pig eyes bulged like wet, white marbles; his face went from red to purple to black. Finally, just when Bill feared he could apply his stranglehold no longer, Landry gave up the ghost. He slumped dead into the sand. His heels scratched twice, and it was over.

Bill started to rise, groaned, stumbled back onto his knees.

"Jesus, I could use a drink," he informed the landscape.

Then the sand hills started spinning out of control, and a badly bleeding Bill Hickok passed out on top of the murdering butcher he had just killed.

"Just a little bit more," Elena Vargas told Bill soothingly. "Be brave. This will sting a little."

Wild Bill, bare to the waist, lay on his stomach across a bench in one of the passenger coaches. Josh watched Elena carefully apply Calomel lotion to the last of his lacerations; she had just spent a painstaking two hours cleaning the sand from them.

"All that sand saved your life," she told Bill. "It stopped the bleeding until clotting took over. You'll still need a doctor, though, when we get to Cheyenne. Some of these cuts are deep."

"That won't be long," Josh said. "The rescue party from Fort Robinson has been spotted to our south."

Among the passengers crowded around Bill was the fox-faced Randolph Bodmer. He had hovered close ever since Josh and a few other men had brought Bill back.

Bill caught Josh's eye and gave him a little half-wink, reminding him of the story they'd prepared.

"Too bad about Professor Vogel," Bill said. "But the way Indians kill a white man, there's no point going back for the body. It won't be pretty."

Bodmer's eyes caught sparks at this welcome news about Vogel, his chief competitor. Now Josh gut-hooked their fish by adding:

"The refrigeration compressor is all right, though. If the buckboard hadn't busted an axle, we'd've brought it back. It's safe for now. We left it in a little bottom beside the trail."

"We'll get it later," Bill agreed. Josh couldn't help a little sting of jealousy at the way Bill was obviously enjoying Elena's gentle hands on his body. And despite his pain, the frontiersman grinned when Bodmer slipped out of the car— never to be seen by white men again, as it turned out. Josh knew the greedy bastard had taken the bait. But all he would find waiting for him along that trail were Sioux warriors.

"What will they do to him?" Josh asked Bill later when they were alone.

"They'll bury him up to his neck in an anthill," Bill replied calmly. "Then soak his head with honey. Takes those ants hours to kill you, and the screams don't stop."

As much as he hated Bodmer, Josh turned green at the prospect.

"Don't worry," Bill added. "He could get lucky. Lots of times, a bear comes along first and rips your head off quick for the honey."

* * *

In the end, ironically, it was the public's hunger for Wild Bill stories that ensured rapid, widespread acceptance of "unnatural ice" in America.

The *New York Herald* headline over Josh's front-page story electrified the young country: WILD BILL AND ECCENTRIC INVENTOR SAVE SIOUX NATION!!! Various versions of Josh's story, often "colored up" a bit, even appeared in England and all throughout Europe, where novels about Hickok had already been translated into eleven languages so far. Even among the haughty French, *le Bill* was all the rage.

As for Vogel's financial backers, their gamble paid off in spades. Thanks to the publicity generated about Wild Bill and the Ice Train, hospital orders alone for the new refrigeration compressor gave the new Omaha factory a two-year backlog of work.

Concerning the now missing Bodmer, Josh realized it was actually merciful for the businessman that he was killed before he had to see his fortunes lost. As his legal fiancée, Elena inherited Bodmer's remaining wealth. Even after his ice business went bankrupt, enough cash would remain to ensure that Elena lived comfortably for the rest of her life. Josh figured she had earned it.

The one person Josh had forgotten about, in all this excitement, was Calamity Jane. But not long after the Ice Train limped into Cheyenne for repairs, Jane proved *she* hadn't forgotten about Wild Bill.

Bill, Josh, and the professor had taken a suite of rooms in Cheyenne's Grand Teton Hotel.

Elena had a room at the end of their hallway. This layover was expected to last about a week while Bill recuperated and further repairs were made to the Ice Train before it resumed its tour.

On their third day in Cheyenne, Bill roused himself from bed, bathed, shaved, and donned his best suit.

"You're going to visit Elena," Josh said, making it more of an accusation than a question.

Bill was about to reply when a voice like gravel shifting called out from the hallway outside: "Yoo-hoo! Bill? Wild Bill? I know you're in here somewhere, darlin'!"

Josh watched his mentor turn green as old brass.

"Wild Bill? I got your flowers in Kansas City, Bill. You *do* know the way straight to a gal's heart, you charmer! And that young buck you sent to deliver 'em was purty enough to eat!"

Bill was on the verge of panic, his eyes those of a trapped deer. Jane's voice was getting closer.

"Bill? That poam you wrote on the card was purty, too! You romantic devil!"

Bill's eyes looked murder at Josh. "What poem, you little shit? I told you just to sign my name."

Josh flushed. "It wasn't anything romantic," he insisted. "Just a line from Shakespeare I threw in to make it sound a little fancier."

"*What* line?"

"Just the line 'Let us not to the marriage of true minds admit impediments.' Nothing romantic, Bill, honest!"

By now Bill was livid. "Kid, you're telling me

you used the word 'marriage'? You used *that* word to her and signed *my* name?"

Josh backed away. Bill looked so murderous in that moment.

"Yoo-hoo! Bill? I'll find you, honey bunch! You can run, but you can't hide forever!"

By now, Calamity Jane was almost at their door.

"Kid," Bill said desperately, "*you* got me into this one. Now you better get me out of it, or that Quaker ma of yours will be wearing funeral black."

The doorknob rattled. Bill flew into the room where Vogel was sleeping and shut the door. Josh screwed up his courage and opened the door to face the grinning, indomitable Calamity Jane.

"Jane," he greeted her in a weak voice. "Wild Bill isn't here right now. But—but could *I* buy you a drink?"

Jane's homely face lit up like a sparkler. "Would a cow lick Lot's wife? *C'mon*, you purty little critter. A lonely gal needs a little comfort, and you'll do just fine!"

Even as she tugged him eagerly into the hallway, the doomed Josh could have sworn he heard Bill chuckle behind him.

CHEYENNE

DOUBLE EDITION
JUDD COLE

One man's heroic search for a world he can call his own.

Arrow Keeper. A Cheyenne raised among pioneers, Matthew Hanchon has never known anything but distrust. The settlers brand him a savage, and when Matthew realizes that his adopted parents will suffer for his sake, he flees into the wilderness—where he'll need a warrior's courage if he hopes to survive.

And in the same volume...

Death Chant. When Matthew returns to the Cheyenne, he doesn't find the acceptance he seeks. The Cheyenne can't fully trust any who were raised in the ways of the white man. Forced to prove his loyalty, Matthew faces the greatest challenge he has ever known.

___4280-0 · $4.99 US/$5.99 CAN

Dorchester Publishing Co., Inc.
P.O. Box 6640
Wayne, PA 19087-8640

CHEYENNE

JUDD COLE

Follow the adventures of Touch the Sky as he searches for a world he can call his own!

#3: Renegade Justice. When his adopted white parents fall victim to a gang of ruthless outlaws, Touch the Sky swears to save them—even if it means losing the trust he has risked his life to win from the Cheyenne.

__3385-2 $3.50 US/$4.50 CAN

#4: Vision Quest. While seeking a mystical sign from the Great Spirit, Touch the Sky is relentlessly pursued by his enemies. But the young brave will battle any peril that stands between him and the vision of his destiny.

__3411-5 $3.50 US/$4.50 CAN

CHEYENNE

Double Edition:
Pathfinder/ Buffalo Hiders
JUDD COLE

Pathfinder. Touch the Sky never forgot the kindness of the settlers, and tried to help them whenever possible. But an old friend's request to negotiate a treaty between the Cheyenne and gold miners brings the young brave face-to-face with a cunning warrior. If Touch the Sky can't defeat his new enemy, the territory will never again be safe for pioneers. *And in the same action-packed volume...*

Buffalo Hiders. Once, mighty herds of buffalo provided the Cheyenne with food, clothing and skins for shelter. Then the white hunters appeared and the slaughter began. Still, few herds remain, and Touch the Sky swears he will protect them. But two hundred veteran mountain men and Indian killers are bent on wiping out the remaining buffalo—and anyone who stands in their way.

___4413-7 $4.99 US/$5.99 CAN

Dorchester Publishing Co., Inc.
P.O. Box 6640
Wayne, PA 19087-8640

Please add $1.75 for shipping and handling for the first book and $.50 for each book thereafter. NY, NYC, and PA residents, please add appropriate sales tax. No cash, stamps, or C.O.D.s. All orders shipped within 6 weeks via postal service book rate. Canadian orders require $2.00 extra postage and must be paid in U.S. dollars through a U.S. banking facility.

Name_____
Address_____
City_____State_____Zip_____
I have enclosed $_____ in payment for the checked book(s).
Payment <u>must</u> accompany all orders. ☐ Please send a free catalog.
CHECK OUT OUR WEBSITE! www.dorchesterpub.com

CHEYENNE

Spirit Path
Mankiller
Judd Cole

Spirit Path. The mighty Cheyenne trust their tribe's shaman to protect them against great sickness and bloody defeat. A rival accuses Touch the Sky of bad medicine, and if he can't prove the claim false, he'll come to a brutal end.

And in the same action-packed volume . . .

Mankiller. A fierce warrior, Touch the Sky can outfight, outwit, and outlast any enemy. Yet the fearsome Cherokee brave named Mankiller can snap a man's neck as easily as a reed, and he is determined to count coup on Touch the Sky.

___4445-5 $4.99 US/$5.99 CAN

Dorchester Publishing Co., Inc.
P.O. Box 6640
Wayne, PA 19087-8640

KIT CARSON

The frontier adventures of a true American legend.

#2: Ghosts of Lodore. When Kit finds himself hurtling down the Green River into an impossibly high canyon, his first worry is to find a way out—until he comes face-to-face with a primitive Indian tribe preparing for a battle in which, one way or another, he will have to take sides.

___4325-4 $3.99 US/$4.99 CAN

#1: The Colonel's Daughter. Kit Carson's courage and strength as an Indian fighter have earned him respect throughout the West. And when the daughter of a Missouri colonel is kidnapped, Kit is determined to find her—even if he has to risk his life to do it!

___4295-9 $3.99 US/$4.99 CAN

Dorchester Publishing Co., Inc.
P.O. Box 6640
Wayne, PA 19087-8640

Please add $1.75 for shipping and handling for the first book and $.50 for each book thereafter. NY, NYC, and PA residents, please add appropriate sales tax. No cash, stamps, or C.O.D.s. All orders shipped within 6 weeks via postal service book rate. Canadian orders require $2.00 extra postage and must be paid in U.S. dollars through a U.S. banking facility.

Name_____
Address_____
City_____State_____Zip_____
I have enclosed $_____ in payment for the checked book(s).
Payment <u>must</u> accompany all orders. ❑ Please send a free catalog.

KIT CARSON

KEELBOAT CARNAGE
DOUG HAWKINS

The untamed frontier is filled with dangers of all kinds—
both natural and man-made—dangers that only the bravest
can survive. And so far Kit Carson has survived them all.
But when he sets out north along the Missouri River he has
no idea what lies ahead. He can't know that the Blackfeet are
out to turn the river red with blood. And when he hitches a
ride on a riverboat, he can't know that keelboat pirates are
waiting just around the bend!

___4411-0 $3.99 US/$4.99 CAN

KIT CARSON

COMANCHE RECKONING

DOUG HAWKINS

There is probably no better tracker in the West than the famous Kit Carson. With his legendary ability to read sign, it is said he can track a mouse over smooth rock. So Kit doesn't expect any trouble when he sets out on the trail of a common thief. But he hasn't counted on a fierce blizzard that seems determined to freeze his bones. Or on a band of furious Comanches led by an old enemy of Kit's—an enemy dead set on revenge.

___4453-6 $3.99 US/$4.99 CAN

LES SAVAGE, JR.
MEDICINE WHEEL

Bob Hogarth arrives in Wyoming's Big Horn Basin with nothing but a small herd of cattle, the result of stubborn scraping and saving back in Texas. He is determined to do better, to own his own ranch, to become a man of substance. But there are lots of folks who aren't too eager to see Hogarth succeed, other ranchers with their own plans for the future, and a mysterious rustler on a barefoot horse. Nobody told Hogarth his dreams would come easy . . . but he knows they are worth fighting for.

___4444-7 $4.50 US/$5.50 CAN

Dorchester Publishing Co., Inc.
P.O. Box 6640
Wayne, PA 19087-8640

WILDERNESS

#24

Mountain Madness

$$\longleftarrow \qquad \longrightarrow$$

David Thompson

When Nate King comes upon a pair of green would-be trappers from New York, he is only too glad to risk his life to save them from a Piegan war party. It is only after he takes them into his own cabin that he realizes they will repay his kindness...with betrayal. When the backshooters reveal their true colors, Nate knows he is in for a brutal battle—with the lives of his family hanging in the balance.

___4399-8 $3.99 US/$4.99 CAN

Dorchester Publishing Co., Inc.
P.O. Box 6640
Wayne, PA 19087-8640

Please add $1.75 for shipping and handling for the first book and $.50 for each book thereafter. NY, NYC, and PA residents, please add appropriate sales tax. No cash, stamps, or C.O.D.s. All orders shipped within 6 weeks via postal service book rate. Canadian orders require $2.00 extra postage and must be paid in U.S. dollars through a U.S. banking facility.

Name_____
Address_____
City_____State_____Zip_____
I have enclosed $_____ in payment for the checked book(s).
Payment <u>must</u> accompany all orders. ❑ Please send a free catalog.
CHECK OUT OUR WEBSITE! www.dorchesterpub.com

WILDERNESS

VENGEANCE TRAIL
DEATH HUNT

The epic struggle for survival in America's untamed West.

Vengeance Trail. When Nate and his mentor, Shakespeare McNair, make enemies of two Flathead Indians, their survival skills are tested as never before.

And in the same action-packed volume....

Death Hunt. Upon the birth of their first child, Nathaniel King and his wife are overjoyed. But their delight turns to terror when Nate accompanies the men of Winona's tribe on a deadly buffalo hunt. If King doesn't return, his family is sure to perish.

___4297-5 $4.99 US/$5.99 CAN

WILDERNESS DOUBLE EDITION

SAVE $$$!

Savage Rendezvous by David Thompson. In 1828, the Rocky Mountains are an immense, unsettled region through which few white men dare travel. Only courageous mountain men like Nathaniel King are willing to risk the unknown dangers for the freedom the wilderness offers. But while attending a rendezvous of trappers and fur traders, King's freedom is threatened when he is accused of murdering several men for their money. With the help of his friend Shakespeare McNair, Nate has to prove his innocence. For he has not cast off the fetters of society to spend the rest of his life behind bars.

And in the same action-packed volume...

Blood Fury by David Thompson. On a hunting trip, young Nathaniel King stumbles onto a disgraced Crow Indian. Attempting to regain his honor, Sitting Bear places himself and his family in great peril, for a war party of hostile Utes threatens to kill them all. When the savages wound Sitting Bear and kidnap his wife and daughter, Nathaniel has to rescue them or watch them perish. But despite his skill in tricking unfriendly Indians, King may have met an enemy he cannot outsmart.

__4208-8 $4.99 US/$5.99 CAN

Dorchester Publishing Co., Inc.
P.O. Box 6640
Wayne, PA 19087-8640

Please add $1.75 for shipping and handling for the first book and $.50 for each book thereafter. NY, NYC, and PA residents, please add appropriate sales tax. No cash, stamps, or C.O.D.s. All orders shipped within 6 weeks via postal service book rate. Canadian orders require $2.00 extra postage and must be paid in U.S. dollars through a U.S. banking facility.

Name_____
Address_____
City_____State_____Zip_____
I have enclosed $_____ in payment for the checked book(s).
Payment <u>must</u> accompany all orders. ❑ Please send a free catalog.